FICTION TEACHER'S GUIDE

Series Editor Katherine Frost
Activity sheets and assessment Debbie Croft, Denise Pilinis

Acknowledgements

The authors and publishers would like to express their special thanks to the following people and schools for their assistance in evaluating *Fast Lane*:
Jill Canning and Rebecca Tyrrell of Fischer Family Trust
Carolyn Harvey
Andrea Kerr
Shirley Thornton
Amy Wilson and the pupils of Primrose Lane Primary School
Judith Graham and the pupils of Littlemead Primary School
Jo Jennings and the pupils of Ninelands Primary School
Diane Rougvie and the pupils of Rye Oak Primary School
Sharman Wood and the pupils of Hawkedon Primary School
Adele Whiteley and the pupils of Pudsey Primrose Hill Primary School

Thanks also to Catch Up (Caxton Turst), Fischer Family Trust and Marie Clay (*An Observation of Early Literacy Achievement*, Heinemann Education New Zealand, 2002).

First published in 2007 by Cengage Learning Australia
www.cengage.com.au

Text by Debbie Croft, Denise Pilinis, Katherine Frost, Rebecca Tyrrell, Hayley Davies-Edwards and Iain Campbell.

Text © 2007 Cengage Learning Australia Pty Ltd ABN 14058280149
(incorporated in Victoria) (pages 3-25, 52-108, CD-Rom downloadable activity sheets);
© 2008 Nelson Thornes Ltd (pages 26-51)

Illustrations © 2007 Cengage Learning Australia Pty Ltd ABN 14058280149
(incorporated in Victoria)

The rights of Debbie Croft, Denise Pilinis, Katherine Frost, Rebecca Tyrrell, Hayley Davies-Edwards and Iain Campbell to be identified as authors of this work have been asserted by them in accordance with the Copyright, Designs and Patents Act 1988.

All rights reserved. No part of this publication may be reproduced or transmitted in any form or by any means, electronic or mechanical, including photocopy, recording or any information storage and retrieval system, without permission in writing from the publisher or under licence from the Copyright Licensing Agency Limited, of Saffron House, 6-10 Kirby Street, London EC1N 8TS.

Any person who commits any unauthorised act in relation to this publication may be liable to criminal prosecution and civil claims for damages.

This edition published in 2008 under the imprint of:
Nelson Thornes Ltd
Delta Place
27 Bath Road
CHELTENHAM
GL53 7TH
United Kingdom

08 09 10 11 12 / 10 9 8 7 6 5 4 3 2 1

A catalogue record for this book is available from the British Library

978-1-4085-0220-4

Series editor: Katherine Frost
Editors: Maoliosa Kelly, Mary Mackill, Frances Ridley

Cover images: (front) Marten Coombe; (back top) Ned Culic; (back bottom) Melissa Webb

Design and page make-up by Anna Stasinska and Karen Young

Teacher's Guide printed by Zrinski (Croatia)
CD-ROM printed by EPC (United Kingdom)

Contents

Introducing *Fast Lane*	**4**
Components	4
Who can use *Fast Lane*?	5
Research	5
Ways to use *Fast Lane*	**6**
Individual and small group intervention	6
Guided reading	6
Withdrawal	6
Making the intervention effective	6
Genres	**7**
Curriculum links	7
Fiction narrative genres	8
How to use *Fast Lane*	**10**
Initial Placement on the *Fast Lane* programme	10
While in a *Fast Lane* band	10
Moving from one *Fast Lane* band to another	11
Leaving the *Fast Lane* programme	11
Books	**12**
Matching pupils to text	12
Levelling	12
Mini audio CDs	13
Design	**14**
Fast Lane fiction books	14
Reading guidance and activities	**16**
Activity sheets	**18**
Assessment	**19**
Band Placement Sheet	19
Reading Record	19
Taking a Reading Record	20
Reading Record (sample)	22
Analysis of sample	23
Other methods of assessment	23
Phonics Assessment	23
Frequently Used Words Assessment	24
Comprehension Assessment	24
Pro formas	**25**
Fast Lane and primary intervention	**26**
Case study: using *Fast Lane* with Hi-Five	27
Fast Lane matching chart	28
Fast Lane and secondary intervention	**29**
Using *Fast Lane* as a secondary intervention scheme	29
Using *Fast Lane* alongside other secondary intervention schemes	30
Fast Lane and other Curricula	**32**
Fast Lane and Scotland	32
Fast Lane and Northern Ireland	33
Fast Lane fiction titles (Yellow to Emerald/levels 6 to 25)	**34**
Assessment sheets	**52**
Level 6 Yellow	52
Level 9 Blue	58
Level 12 Green	64
Level 15 Orange	70
Level 17 Turquoise	76
Level 19 Purple	82
Level 21 Gold	88
Level 23 Silver	94
Level 25 Emerald	100
Pro formas	**106**
Reading Record	106
Reading Graph	107
Weekly Individual Literacy Plan	108
Practical activities	
Making the most of phonic opportunities	109–110
Making the most of frequently used words	111–112

Introducing Fast Lane

Fast Lane is a high-interest, low-readability, levelled intervention programme aimed at middle years pupils who need a high level of support to improve their literacy achievement. The programme focuses on developing the literacy skills of these pupils by providing them with high-interest books at their appropriate reading level. A complete and balanced programme, *Fast Lane* is designed to meet the literacy needs of all pupils, including English Language Learners and pupils with additional needs.

Fast Lane has been developed in response to teachers' need for appropriate reading material for struggling readers. It is widely recognised that these pupils require the following:

- Books that are at their interest level as well as their reading level
- Content that is relevant to the themes and topics being studied in the classroom
- Finely graded books to support reading development
- Books that look 'age-appropriate' in terms of design and size
- A range of text types and genres to model the different social purposes of text and the ways in which it can be presented
- Activities that are related to their specific area of need
- A programme that has a consistent structure and is routine-based
- Books that emphasise visual literacy
- Audio support to model fluent reading.

Components

Fast Lane consists of 142 titles for pupils who need levelled texts with age-appropriate content. The programme is consistent and supportive and features repetition and reinforcement of learned reading strategies.

The *Fast Lane* books are levelled and banded using the PM levelling system, with adaptations that take into account the needs of older struggling readers. The PM levelling system is based on the same colour bands as Reading Recovery book bands.

The components of the scheme are:

- 142 reading books, each with its own audio CD (71 fiction, 71 non-fiction)
- 2 Teacher's Guides (*Fast Lane* Fiction Teacher's Guide and *Fast Lane* Non-Fiction Teacher's Guide, each with a CD-ROM of activities)

The reading books are organised as follows:

- *Fast Lane* Yellow band (levels 6-8): 9 fiction, 9 non-fiction
- *Fast Lane* Blue band (levels 9-11): 9 fiction, 9 non-fiction
- *Fast Lane* Green band (levels 12-14): 9 fiction, 9 non-fiction
- *Fast Lane* Orange band (levels 15-16): 8 fiction, 8 non-fiction
- *Fast Lane* Turquoise band (levels 17-18): 8 fiction, 8 non-fiction
- *Fast Lane* Purple band (levels 19-20): 8 fiction, 8 non-fiction
- *Fast Lane* Gold band (levels 21-22): 8 fiction, 8 non-fiction
- *Fast Lane* Silver band (levels 23-24): 8 fiction, 8 non-fiction
- *Fast Lane* Emerald band (level 25): 4 fiction, 4 non-fiction

These are the six titles from Yellow level 6, the first of three levels in the Yellow band. Each level contains a mixture of fiction and non-fiction books, each with an audio CD attached to the front cover. The Fiction Teacher's Guide and the Non-Fiction Teacher's Guide contain assessments for each *Fast Lane* band and pro formas. Both have an accompanying CD-ROM of activities for each book.

Who can use *Fast Lane*?

Fast Lane has been developed for pupils in the middle years of learning who are struggling with literacy. The pupil may have a learning difficulty, be disengaged or simply require further reading practice. Whatever the reason, these books aim to increase reading ability and confidence by appealing to the pupil's interest level and reading level.

The programme has also been structured to assist English language learners in developing proficiency in reading. The language structures and visual elements are highly supportive and have been trialled extensively with pupils from Non English Speaking Backgrounds and English Language Learners.

Research

The *Fast Lane* programme has been developed using extensive independent research by staff from the Department of Language, Literacy and Arts Education at the University of Melbourne.

The research team at the University of Melbourne designed and conducted experimental research in tandem with the development of this programme. The programme was trialled with the following groups of pupils:

- English Language Learners from both low and high socio-economic backgrounds
- English Speaking Background pupils from both low and high socio-economic backgrounds.

This robust and experimental research has been used to inform and refine the programme. The experimental nature of the research involved the use of control groups. The research team presented summative findings at various stages, which were invaluable in developing *Fast Lane* to the highest standard.

In its Final Report, dated March 2006, the University of Melbourne stated in their overall conclusion:

> *There are very few resources currently available on the Australian market that are specifically designed to support struggling readers with low literacy levels in the middle years of schooling. On this basis, the* Fast Lane *reading intervention programme is quite innovative and even groundbreaking, as distinct from the majority of Australian commercially produced reading resources today.* Fast Lane *is therefore a unique and very commendable product aimed at supporting struggling readers in the middle years of schooling.*

The Report goes on to emphasise that "it is well known that reading material for pupils who have difficulty reading is often unmotivating ... *Fast Lane* is a welcome and very commendable break from what dominates in the market for such readers".

In addition, *Fast Lane* has been extensively trialled with excellent feedback in a range of UK schools with children of a range of ages and reading ability. It is also being piloted with a number of reading intervention programmes. The trialling research confirmed that the texts are highly engaging, even for the most reluctant reader, with very accurate levelling and relevant and appealing subject links.

Assessing a pupil using the reading record.

Ways to use Fast Lane

Fast Lane can be used as an individualised programme that can run in any primary or secondary classroom in the middle years. It also allows for small group work to suit the different educational contexts within schools. *Fast Lane* forms the basis of explicit and systematic instruction to ensure the development of literacy skills. Pupils of this programme must also have extensive amounts of partner, group and independent reading of instructional and independent level books to further support their literacy development while on the programme.

Fast Lane has been designed to work in the following educational contexts:

- In individual and small group intervention
- In guided reading groups within the classroom
- As a withdrawal programme.

Individual and small group intervention

Pupils may operate in the classroom on a fully individualised reading programme. *Fast Lane* is systematic in its approach and pupils can work on the programme autonomously during the literacy session or during normal classroom time by reading *Fast Lane* books that relate to the theme or topic being taught. The non-fiction texts link to themes covered in many areas of the curriculum.

Guided reading

Fast Lane can be implemented in the classroom as a part of reading groups. Pupils may be grouped according to their reading level and participate in guided reading using the books from the programme.

Withdrawal

Pupils may be withdrawn by a specialist reading teacher or by a support staff member. This withdrawal can be done with groups of pupils as well as individuals.

Making the intervention effective

To guarantee that intervention using *Fast Lane* is effective, it is recommended that pupils engage in the programme for 15 to 30 minutes, three to five days a week. The following will also help to make the intervention effective:

- The involvement of teachers, well-briefed support staff and assistants
- Personalised assessment-based instruction
- Adequate time for pupils to practise the skills they need to develop
- Small adult to pupil ratios
- Commitment to the intervention programme.

Guided reading using the *Fast Lane* programme.

Genres

Integral to a successful literacy approach is exposing pupils to the different types of text that they are likely to use in other curriculum subjects.

Fast Lane aims to show pupils that there are a number of different types of text. It also shows that these text types have different purposes, are structured in different ways and consist of different grammatical features. A detailed grid showing fiction text types can be found on pages 8-9.

Fast Lane includes the following fictional narrative genres throughout the series:

- Fantasy stories
- Stories with a familiar setting
- Mystery and adventure stories
- Stories with issues
- Stories set in an imaginary world
- Traditional tales from around the world

 Curriculum links

Fast Lane reading books can be used alongside a range of other curriculum subjects in both primary and secondary classrooms. They can assist teachers in the middle years by developing pupils's literacy skills that are relevant to a particular subject. For example, some of the fiction texts deal with themes relevant to citizenship or history.

The Bully
(turquoise level 18 story with issues)

Buzz sees the Difference
(purple level 19 story set in an imaginary world)

Noises in the Night
(yellow level 6 story with a familiar setting)

The Game
(green level 12 fantasy story)

The Contest
(silver level 23 traditional tale)

Glacier
(turquoise level 18 adventure story)

Fiction narrative genres: organisation and language features

Genre	*Fast Lane* examples	Purpose
Story with a familiar setting	**Noises in the Night** (Yellow level 6) **The Mess** (Yellow level 7) **The Mystery of the Missing Bike** (Yellow level 8) **Dad and Dan Go Camping** (Blue level 10)	To entertain with a story using settings, situations and experience that the listener will recognise.
Fantasy story	**Time Travel: the Dinosaurs** (Blue level 9) **The Game** (Green level 12) **Time Travel: Ship Ahoy!** (Green level 13) **I Wish** (Gold level 22)	To entertain with a story which includes a fantastic or impossible element. It sometimes uses imaginary settings, characters and situations.
Story set in an imaginary world	**Buzz and Zip Get Lost** (Blue level 10) **Gadget Boy Saves the Day** (Turquoise level 17) **Gadget Boy and Kid Fantastic** (Purple level 20)	To entertain with a story set in an imaginary setting, sometimes with normal characters.
Adventure story	**Shark** (Blue level 10) **Jump!** (Blue level 11) **Glacier** (Turquoise level 18) **Mudslide** (Gold level 22) **Shipwreck** (Silver level 24)	To entertain with a story with an unfamiliar setting, with exciting events, but often with normal characters.
Mystery story	**The Mystery of the Missing Bike** (Blue level 10) **Secret Agent** (Green level 14) **Neighbours** (Gold level 21)	To entertain with a story about encountering or resolving a secret, crime or other mysterious event or object.
Story with issues	**Saying Goodbye** (Blue level 11) **Don't Embarrass Me Dad** (Green level 13) **The Bully** (Turquoise level 18) **The Coat** (Purple level 20) **More Like Home** (Emerald level 25)	To entertain with a story, usually with a familiar setting, which addresses an issue which is often relevant to pupils, for example, bullying, peer pressure etc.
Traditional tale (including fables, myths and stories from other cultures)	**The Call of the Wolf** (Green level 12) **The Golden Touch** (Orange level 15) **Mercury and the Woodcutter** (Orange level 16) **The Riddle of the Camel Race** (Gold level 21) **The Contest** (Silver level 23)	A story written or told a long time ago, which has been retold many times since.

Generic text structure	Grammatical patterns	Punctuation patterns
Story has three parts: (1) Orientation - introduces the main characters and setting; (2) Complication - the sequence of events develops a problem for the main character; (3) Resolution - the problem is solved and things return to normal.	• Adjectives and noun phrases to describe: e.g. knobbly, more funny pranks; • Adverbs and phrases of time; • Similes, e.g. like a hurricane; • Time connectives to sequence events through time, e.g. two days later, within seconds; • Written in past tense (with some use of present tense); • Mainly chronological, possible use of time shifts; • Stereotypical characters, settings and events; • Connectives used to shift attention, e.g. meanwhile, or to signal time, e.g. early that morning, or to inject suspense, e.g. suddenly; • Language effects to create impact on the reader such as adverbs, adjectives, precise nouns, expressive verbs, simile and metaphors.	• A mixture of sentence types: complex, compound and short to vary the pace of the text; • Apostrophes to indicate contractions; • Speech marks to indicate actual words spoken; • Punctuation such as an ellipsis to create suspense, or a dash to create a pause in the sentence; • Use of repetition to emphasise actions, e.g. Down, down; • Exclamation mark to express the emotion of the speaker or situation; • Bold font or capitalisation to add extra impact to the situation.
Story has three parts: (1) Orientation; (2) Complication; (3) Resolution - the problem is solved and things return to normal. Often the resolution has a moral or message, for example, good conquers evil, pride comes before a fall etc.	• Written in first or third person; • Written in past tense; • Events in chronological order; • Main participants are often contrasting – e.g. good/bad, clever/foolish, etc. • Use of connectives to signal time, e.g. Early that morning; • Language effects to create impact on the reader, e.g. adverbs, adjectives, expressive verbs, similes; • Some use of repetitive structures, e.g. ...but the first was too big, the second was too small but the third...	

How to use Fast Lane

Initial placement on the Fast Lane programme

Fast Lane is graded in a series of bands, which are broken down further into two or three reading levels.

To place a pupil, he or she needs to be assessed to find their instructional *Fast Lane* band. Initial placement assessment is done by either:

1. **Taking a reading record**

   Two Reading Record Assessments are provided for each *Fast Lane* band – one for a fiction book and one for a non-fiction book from the initial reading level of each *Fast Lane* band (for example, level 6 for *Fast Lane* Yellow band, and level 9 for *Fast Lane* Blue band). It is recommended that the teacher assesses a pupil using both the fiction and non-fiction Reading Record Assessments (although not necessarily at the same time), as strategies for reading fiction and non-fiction books differ. If the pupil scores between 90–94% accuracy and replies to the comprehension questions with appropriate understanding, he or she is reading at his or her instructional reading level and *Fast Lane* band. If the pupil scores 95% or above accuracy and replies correctly to all the questions, he or she could be tried with a book at the next reading level, or, alternatively, tested at the next *Fast Lane* band. If the pupil scores below 90% accuracy, he or she could be tried on a book at the reading level below the *Fast Lane* band, or, alternatively, be tested at a lower *Fast Lane* band. See pages 19–23 for how to take a reading record and how to analyse the results.

2. **Using the other assessment methods**

   (Phonics Assessment, Frequently Used Words Assessment, Comprehension Assessment)
   A score of 70–80% on the Phonics Assessment, the Frequently Used Words Assessment and the Comprehension Assessment is a good indicator of the pupil's instructional reading level. See pages 23–24 for how to use these assessment methods and how to analyse the data collected.

The results of the reading record or other assessment methods should then be entered into the band placement sheet, which are provided for each *Fast Lane* band and can be found on pages 52–105 of this teacher's guide.

The completed assessment will help identify a pupil's particular area of need; for example, meaning (comprehension), structure (vocabulary) or phonics (visual). The teacher can then access appropriate *Fast Lane* activities so the pupil can practise the skill or skills he or she needs to develop to further their reading ability. There are three activity sheets for each book in the series, relating to comprehension, vocabulary and phonics.

While in a Fast Lane band

It is recommended that pupils engage in the *Fast Lane* scheme for 15–30 minutes, three to five days a week. The pupil does not have to read all the books in a level or *Fast Lane* band, but reading a range of books, both fiction and non-fiction, at one level or progressing slowly up through the levels within a *Fast Lane* band, ensures the pupil has plenty of practice before moving on to the next level. Having a breadth of experience at any one *Fast Lane* band will make the transition to the next *Fast Lane* band easier and ensure wider literacy skills are developed.

Instructional reading with a Fast Lane book

For each book in a band or level, it is recommended that the teacher follows these steps:

1. The teacher orientates the pupil to the book. Then the pupil reads the book to the teacher, while the teacher provides appropriate instruction, which could be:
   a) Encouraging the pupil to self-correct
   b) Giving prompts or clues to help with self-correction
   c) Allowing the pupil to check or repeat so he or she can confirm predictions
   d) Asking the pupil 'How do you know?' when he or she decodes a word.

Detailed guidance on the kinds of questions to ask or helpful learning points can be found on the inside back cover of every *Fast Lane* reading book.

2. In addition, the pupil may do all or some of the following in any order:
   a) Complete the activity sheet or sheets (available on the Teacher's Guide CD-ROM) relating to the book they have read, depending on the area of need identified by the teacher
   b) Read the book along with the audio CD
   c) Read the book independently.
3. The pupil reads the same book to the teacher again.
4. The teacher then decides on the next book for the pupil to read.

Moving from one *Fast Lane* band to another

Once a pupil has successfully read books at the different levels within one *Fast Lane* band (reading with both fluency and a high level of accuracy), he or she may be ready to try the next *Fast Lane* band.

To move a pupil from one *Fast Lane* band to the next, assess the pupil using the assessment methods provided for the next *Fast Lane* band, in exactly the same way as described on the previous page. Once again, if the pupil scores between 90–94% on the reading record (or 70–80% using the other assessment methods), he or she is ready to read the books in the new *Fast Lane* band. If the pupil scores below 90%, you may wish to keep the pupil at his or her present *Fast Lane* band and level; if the pupil scores above 95% accuracy you wish to try him or her at a higher level within the new *Fast Lane* band.

The results of the reading record or other assessment methods should then be entered into the band placement sheet provided for each *Fast Lane* band and which can be found on pages 52–105 of this teacher's guide.

As with initial placement, the completed assessment will help identify a pupil's particular area of need and the teacher can then access the appropriate *Fast Lane* activity sheets so the pupil can practise the skill or skills he or she needs to develop. Three activity sheets for each book in the series, relating to comprehension, vocabulary and phonics, are provided.

Leaving the *Fast Lane* programme

Once a pupil is successfully reading books in the *Fast Lane* Emerald band, he or she may be ready to leave the scheme. As with initial placement or to move between *Fast Lane* bands, the pupil should achieve an accuracy rate of 95% or above on the reading record (or above 80% using the other assessment methods) to be ready to leave the scheme.

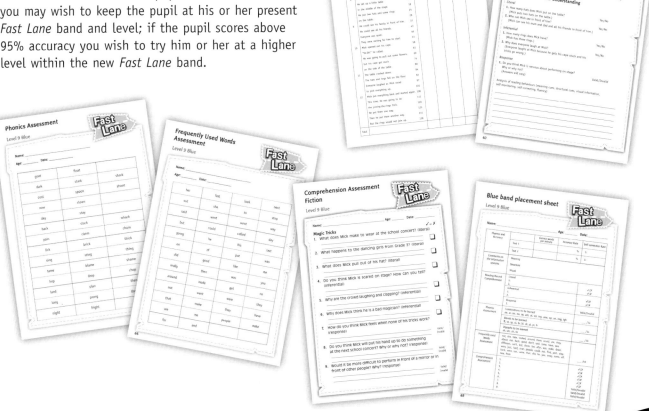

Books

Matching pupils to text

There are few tasks more challenging for teachers than reaching struggling readers in the middle years of schooling. Low-achieving readers may go through school never engaging with challenging texts appropriate to their age level. These struggling readers do not have the chance to talk with their peers about the material that their reading contains as it is not linked to anything that the rest of the pupils are reading.

McCormack, R.L. and Paratore, J.R. (editors),
After Early Intervention, Then What?
Teaching Struggling Readers in Grades 3 and Beyond,
International Reading Association, Inc.,
Delaware, 2003

The books within *Fast Lane* range from 16 to 24 pages, allowing pupils to feel a sense of achievement at having read a whole book in one reading session. The *Fast Lane* texts have been carefully written using a slow introduction of new vocabulary, but with content appropriate for older readers. The new vocabulary is reinforced throughout the text and succeeding books. *Fast Lane* books do not look different from other reading materials in the classroom. They will have as much appeal for fluent readers as they do for struggling readers. The fiction and non-fiction texts differ in appearance to reinforce the idea that not all reading texts look the same.

The 'traditional' appearance of a book is vitally important for pupils whose self-esteem as readers may be lacking. All the texts within *Fast Lane* have a contemporary appearance that reflects the high-interest content. Careful consideration has been given to page layout so that pupils know exactly where to go to start accessing information. Deliberate line breaks occur in levels 6 to 16 to help encourage good fluency and phrasing.

Levelling

In order to access the Level 6 texts, pupils will be expected to know a bank of frequently used words. This word list is a culmination of words taken from a number of well-known sources. To ensure that pupils are given every opportunity to succeed in their reading, the introduction of new words is one new word for every 16 known words (1:16).

Newly introduced words are a combination of frequently used words and interest words. The interest words have been carefully chosen to develop the subject-specific vocabulary that pupils require to read for meaning and to participate in class discussion.

Unlike levelled reading programmes for younger pupils, *Fast Lane* introduces grammatical structures like complex sentences and contractions at the earliest levels. Given that older pupils have more sophisticated oral language, the language structures of the texts reflect this. To support this approach, extensive trialling with pupils found that they were automatically saying 'didn't' when the text actually read 'did not'.

Teachers familiar with schemes with PM or Reading Recovery Book Bands Yellow and Blue will notice that the *Fast Lane* books at these bands have considerably more words (about 350). This is because the *Fast Lane* research demonstrated that a struggling reader aged 8 or more will achieve a reading rate of 35 words per minute or more. In order to gain meaningful reading practice the struggling reader needs to be engaged in sustained reading for about ten minutes.

The books within the series have been given individual levels that coincide with the following colour bands:

Levels 6–8	Yellow
Levels 9–11	Blue
Levels 12–14	Green
Levels 15–16	Orange
Levels 17–18	Turquoise
Levels 19–20	Purple
Levels 21–22	Gold
Levels 23–24	Silver
Level 25	Emerald

Levelling indicators

Like all pupils, struggling readers want to be reading books that look the same as those of their peers. *Fast Lane* books feature subtle levelling indicators, allowing teachers to recognise each book's level at a glance, without making the level obvious to pupils.

Colour level bar

The spine of each book features a coloured bar representing the title's colour band and level. For example, levels 6, 7 and 8 are part of the Yellow colour band, so these books feature a yellow bar. This bar varies in length according to the level of the book: the bar of a level 6 book goes one-third of the way up the spine; the bar of a level 7 book goes two-thirds of the way up the spine; and the bar of a level 8 book goes all the way up the spine.

Book level

The individual level of each book appears in small type above the barcode on the back cover.

Mini audio CDs

All *Fast Lane* books are accompanied by a mini audio CD. Audio-assisted reading provides an excellent model of fluent reading, whereby pupils can learn how a reader's voice, using fluency, phrasing and expression, can help written text to make sense.

The CDs have a mix of male and female voices as well as various subtle sound effects. These sound effects add interest to the recording without distracting the reader, interrupting the flow of the text or overwhelming the clarity of the recording.

The mini audio CDs can be used to assist with pupils' fluency and phrasing. When the pupil has read the written text, have the pupil listen to the audio CD and practise reading the text along with the voice. The pupil should be encouraged to have a number of readings of the same text.

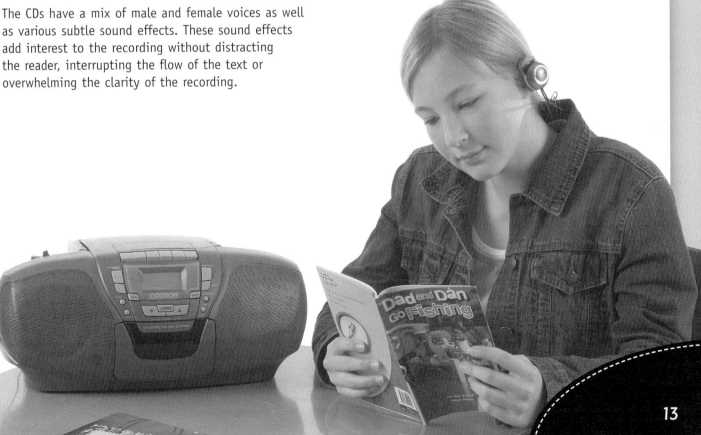

Design

Fast Lane has been developed to give pupils exposure to the types of texts that they will be increasingly faced with as they move through the upper years of school. *Fast Lane* also recognises the fact that pupils are becoming increasingly exposed to visual forms of communication and therefore need the skills to interpret information in a variety of formats.

The *Fast Lane* fiction books have been carefully written to provide a variety of different styles and genres that will appeal to older readers. They have clearly defined characters with compelling storylines. Some characters, like Buzz, Zip and Mick the Magician, recur at different levels of the series.

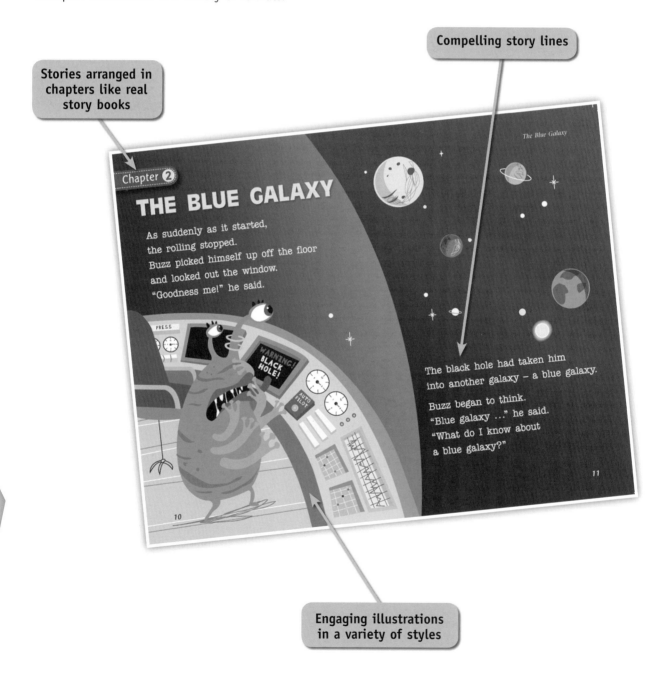

Stories arranged in chapters like real story books

Compelling story lines

Engaging illustrations in a variety of styles

Supportive page layouts

Appropriate sentence structures

Some books use different ways to present a story, like this graphic novel

Reading guidance and activities

The *Fast Lane* teaching notes have been carefully structured to provide teachers and well-briefed support assistants with clear and explicit notes for each reading book in the *Fast Lane* programme. The teaching notes are designed to highlight the key learning features of each book, including vocabulary, text type, visual literacy, phonic, grammatical, text and punctuation patterns. The teaching notes are found inside the front and back covers of each reading book.

The teaching notes are highly supportive and will help both teachers and pupils gain maximum benefit from the *Fast Lane* scheme.

The teaching notes are divided into two parts. The first part, on the inside front cover, provides key literacy information about the book, while the second part, on the inside back cover, provides suggested guidance and activities to maximise the learning from opportunities the book presents. This part is split into three sections: Before reading, During reading and After reading.

Key information

These are key facts for the teacher who is looking to quickly access and place the reading book alongside other reading resources or into planning.

Word count

Text type or **genre**

Cross-curricular links to other subjects

Words in context words which are likely to be unfamiliar or newly introduced in the text

Phonic opportunities, with examples from the books given, which can be used for a range of phonic activities outlined in the Teacher's Guides.

Frequently used words which are used repeatedly in the book in order to familiarise the pupil with them. Activity suggestions are given in the back of the teacher's guides for pupils to practise these words.

Dad's Trick

Word count
536

Text type
Story in a familiar setting

Cross-curricular links
Science (the human body), Citizenship (local community, tolerance)

Words in context
assistant, disappeared, enemy, infected, instructions, meaningful, sca... supermarket, ugliest, understood

Phonic opportunities
grapheme *ea* (cr*ea*m p.4, m*ea*ningful p.6, r*ea*ched p.12, inst*ea*d p.15, *area* p.22); phoneme /u/ (*one* p.4, *front* p.8, *under* p.10, some*one* p... instr*u*ctions p.22)

Frequently used words
after, first, front, own, right, seen, some, thought, under

Dad's Trick
(Orange level 15)

inside front cover

Before reading

These are suggested discussion points the teacher or assistant could use to help introduce the text to the pupils before starting to read.

- A short statement of the purpose of the text, to help the pupils understand why they are reading it.
- Getting the pupils to identify and respond to the book's text type and predict content, through looking at the cover, title, and its visual features.
- Relating to pupils' background knowledge and familiarity with the book's topic and concepts.

During reading

This is a summary of what to look for in the pupils' reading, including reading strategies and the learning opportunities inherent in the text.

- A short description of the observed reading process required for the book.
- Fluency and pronunciation points which may arise during the course of the reading.
- Prompts for highlighting particular vocabulary opportunities.
- Prompts to check the pupils' comprehension of the book, including literal (L), inferential (I) and response (R) questions.
- Prompts to observe how the visual features of the book help the book's purpose and relate to the text.
- Identification of possible grammatical and text features of the book which are characteristic of its type and purpose.

After reading

This section outlines activities which the pupils could do to support their learning, including:

- Using the mini audio CD to help practise fluency and phrasing in reading.
- A short extension activity to build on what they have learned with regards to the topic or structure of the book, often with an emphasis on writing.
- Prompts to use the reading book's specific CD-ROM activities to support assessment or reinforcement of the pupils' reading skills.

Reading guidance and activities

Before reading

- The purpose of the text is to tell a story about a girl who gets her first pimple and how, in a supermarket, her dad comes to the rescue to avoid her becoming embarrassed in front of some children she knows.
- Draw attention to the title, illustrations and chapter headings. What type of book is this? How do you know? Where is it set? Do you think it's a modern story? Why?
- Discuss what pimples are, who usually gets them and how they can be embarrassing for the person who has them.

During reading

- Ask the children to read aloud, and observe their phrasing and fluency, particularly when reading short sentences.
- At appropriate points during the reading of the whole book, stop and ask questions.
- Check understanding of unfamiliar vocabulary. What does *ugliest* mean? What is the root word? What happens when something gets *infected*?
- Check children's understanding of the text. (L) Who is Lauren's worst enemy? (I) Why does Lauren's face turn red when she is at the check-out? (R) If you had been with Lauren, how would you have tried to help?
- Look at the illustrations, especially those in which the characters' expressions change when Dad makes out the pimple cream is for him. How does that help the reader to know what they are thinking?
- Discuss how the story starts. How does Connor's reaction towards her first pimple make Lauren feel? Do you think she would have been less embarrassed at the supermarket if the story hadn't started out that way? Discuss how the opening is used to set up the main theme of a story.
- Together, identify some adjectives and discuss how they affect the nouns, e.g. *ugliest* (p.4), *meaningful* (p.6), *loud* (p.12), *worst* (p.16), *infected* (p.22).

After reading

- Children could listen to the mini-CD recording and practise reading the text along with the voice.
- Discuss situations when the children have felt embarrassed. They could use these as the basis for story writing.
- If the children need support for meaning, structure and visual skills, printable activities are available on the *Fiction Teacher's Guide* CD-ROM.

inside back cover

Activity sheets

The activity sheets for the *Fast Lane* fiction books are found on the CD-ROM accompanying this teacher's guide.

The activities in *Fast Lane* have been specifically designed to link in with the assessment. When the pupil's area of need has been determined, the teacher can access activity sheets that the pupil can use to further practise the skill (or skills) that needs developing.

There are three activities for each book in the *Fast Lane* series, relating to the following areas:

- Comprehension (meaning)
- Vocabulary (structure)
- Phonics (visual)

The activities in each level remain consistent. This has been done to assist the teacher in reducing the amount of teaching time required to explain the activities and to support the pupil as he or she becomes familiar with the layout and expectations of each activity.

How to select the appropriate activity for each pupil

The assessment drives the selection of activities for each pupil. If a pupil's assessment shows that he or she is experiencing difficulty with meaning (comprehension), then it is recommended that the pupil work on the comprehension activities to help strengthen this area of reading. If the pupil is assessed as requiring practice with visual (phonics) information, then he or she should do the phonics activities. If the pupil is assessed as needing further consolidation in the area of structure, then he or she should do the vocabulary activities.

Downloadable activity sheets for Dad's Trick

Assessment

The assessment materials can be found on pages 52–108 of this teacher's guide.

To place a pupil on the correct level for reading instruction, professional teacher judgement is paramount. The teacher must determine not only the pupil's instructional level of reading, but also his or her knowledge of the three information systems required to be a proficient reader. The proficient reader is able to access and utilise the following three information systems:

- Semantic information (meaning)
- Syntactic information (structure)
- Grapho-phonological information (visual).

The assessment provided for *Fast Lane* helps the teacher to determine the instructional reading level for pupils entering the programme and for those moving through the programme. The assessment also helps the teacher to determine the explicit instruction a pupil requires to master the problem-solving task of reading.

Not all of the assessment sheets need to be done to determine a pupil's instructional reading level. It is suggested that if a reading record is not completed, the pupil should complete *all* the other assessments: the Phonics Assessment, the Frequently Used Words Assessment and the Comprehension Assessment.

As teacher judgement is paramount in determining both the starting point and the movement of pupils through *Fast Lane* levels, each pupil's results must be viewed individually. For example, a pupil may score very well on one assessment sheet but very poorly on another. The teacher's knowledge of each pupil and what the teacher decides to teach next will play an important role in determining both the *Fast Lane* band at which each pupil will begin the programme and when he or she progresses to the next level or *Fast Lane* band.

 Band Placement Sheet

The Band Placement Sheet is used to record assessment data when the pupil is initially placed on the programme. This summary will give teachers a guide as to the level at which the pupil should start. The Band Placement Sheet is also used at the end of each *Fast Lane* band to record pupil assessment results.

This sheet will also assist teachers to determine when a pupil moves up to the next level or *Fast Lane* band. Both sheets provide an ongoing and detailed insight into a pupil's progress throughout the programme.

The band placement sheets drive pupil activity. If the assessment shows that a pupil is having difficulty with meaning (comprehension), then it is recommended that he or she work on comprehension worksheets to help strengthen this area of reading. If the pupil needs work with visual (phonics) information, then he or she should focus on the phonics sheets. If the pupil needs further consolidation in the area of structure, then he or she should work on the vocabulary and/or writing activity sheets.

> Band Placement Sheets can be found in the assessment section (pages 52–108).

 Reading record

It is recommended that teachers using *Fast Lane* use a reading record to determine a pupil's instructional reading level. This is the most effective method by which to determine a pupil's reading level. The reading record will not only indicate the pupil's starting level, it will also indicate the areas in which the pupil is experiencing difficulty. After analysing the reading record, the teacher will know what the teaching focus should be for that particular pupil.

Two Reading Record Assessments are provided for each *Fast Lane* band – one for a fiction book and one for a non-fiction book from the initial reading level of each *Fast Lane* band. Oral comprehension questions are also provided for each Reading Record Assessment. The questions are divided into literal, inferential and response. The Reading Record Assessments can be used to place the pupil on a *Fast Lane* band. It is recommended that the teacher assess the pupil using both Reading Record Assessments (but not necessarily at the same time), as strategies for reading fiction and non-fiction books differ.

> The Reading Record Assessments can be found in the assessment section (pages 52–108).

Taking a reading record

Materials

- 1 copy of the relevant fiction book for the *Fast Lane* band
- 1 copy of the Reading Record
- 1 copy of the Reading Record Assessment for the book
- 1 copy of the Band Placement Sheet.

Implementation

1. The teacher gives the pupil an orientation to the book. During this orientation time (approximately five minutes), the teacher must give the pupil:
   - the title of the book
   - any proper nouns in the text (e.g. names of places)
   - any background concepts the pupil needs to access the text (e.g. a brief outline of the content of the text).

2. The teacher sits near the pupil, and as the pupil reads aloud from his or her copy of the book, the teacher records the pupil's reading behaviour on errors only and notes self-corrections, on the Reading Record (see sample page 22).
   - If a word is substituted, record it and call it an error.

     Substitution: $\frac{went}{want}$ $\left(\frac{child}{text}\right)$

   - If a word is omitted, record it and call it an error.

     Omission: $\frac{-}{very}$

   - If a word is inserted, record it and call it an error.

     Insertion: $\frac{little}{-}$

   - Any modification or assistance the teacher offers should be called an error and noted with a "T" (for teacher).

     Told (T): $\frac{\quad}{thought} \mid T$

   - If the pupil appeals for a word, the teacher should say, "You try it". If unable to continue, record "A" (for appeal), tell the pupil the word and call it an error.

     Appeal (A): $\frac{\quad\mid A}{sometimes \mid}$

   - Self-corrections are not considered as errors when the teacher is completing the reading record – they indicate that the pupil is monitoring meaning as he or she reads.

     Self-correction (SC): $\frac{went}{want} \mid \frac{SC}{\ }$

   - Repetition "R" is not counted as an error, but should be shown above the word that is repeated (as well as the number of repetitions, if more than one). Include an arrow if the pupil goes back over several words.

     Repetition (R): R or ✓✓ R

   - If the pupil is confused, say, "Try that again" "TTA". Put square brackets around the text that caused the confusion. Only count this as an error if the pupil is still confused.

     Try that again: [TTA]

3. The teacher asks the pupil the five oral comprehension questions provided for the book on the Reading Record Assessment sheet. The pupil should have access to the book while answering the questions.

Analysis of data

When the reading record is completed, the teacher analyses the data collected. A pattern will emerge from the analysis that will enable the teacher to draw conclusions about the pupil and decide the pupil's particular teaching focus.

1. The teacher puts a "1" in the first two columns of the reading record beside every error and self-correction. Then the teacher counts the number of errors and self-corrections and records these at the bottom of the first two columns.

2. The teacher calculates the Error Rate (see box "To Calculate Error Rate" below) and the Self-correction Rate (see box "To Calculate Self-correction Rate" on page 21).

To Calculate Error Rate

Divide the number of words read (R.W.) by the number of errors (E).

Running words   150
Errors   15
Error Rate: 1:10

To Calculate Self-correction Rate

1. Add both errors (E) and self-corrections (S.C.) together.
2. Divide by the number of self-corrections.

15 (E) + 5 (S.C.) = 20
20 ÷ 5 = 4
Self-correction Rate: 1:4

3. The teacher uses the table to obtain the Accuracy Rate (see "Reading Level Table" below). Alternatively, the teacher can calculate the Accuracy Rate using the formula (see box "To Calculate Accuracy Rate").

Reading Level Table

Level	Error Rate	Percent Accuracy
Easy	1:200	99.50
Easy	1:100	99
Easy	1:50	98
Easy	1:35	97
Easy	1:25	96
Easy	1:20	95
Instructional	1:17	94
Instructional	1:14	93
Instructional	1:12.5	92
Instructional	1:11.75	91
Instructional	1:10	90
Hard	1:9	89
Hard	1:8	87.5
Hard	1:7	85.5
Hard	1:6	83
Hard	1:5	80
Hard	1:4	76
Hard	1:3	65
Hard	1:2	50

To Calculate Accuracy Rate

1. Divide the Errors by the Running Words and multiply by 100.
2. Take away that number from 100.

$$\frac{E}{R.W.} \times 100 \qquad \frac{15}{150} \times 100 = 10$$

100 − 10 = 90
Accuracy Rate: 90%

4. The teacher categorises each of the pupil's errors and self-corrections according to the information systems the pupil accessed: semantic (meaning), grammatical (structure) and graphological or phonological (visual or sound). On each line where errors or self-corrections occur, the teacher indicates the information systems the pupil has used by circling M, S or V in the Errors MSV column:
   'M' if the pupil was trying to use meaning
   'S' if the pupil was trying to use language structure
   'V' if the pupil was trying to use visual cues.
5. The teacher counts the number of times each information system was used for errors and for self-corrections and records the totals at the bottom of the last two columns. This information gives the teacher insight into the dominant information systems being used by the pupil.
6. The teacher analyses the way in which the pupil answered the five oral comprehension questions, identifying the depth of meaning the pupil has gained from reading the text.
7. The teacher enters the data collected on the Band Placement Sheet.

Results

The teacher can make the following conclusions from the analysis of the data collected from the Reading Record Assessment:

- If the pupil scores between 90–94% accuracy and replies to the comprehension questions with appropriate understanding, the pupil is reading at his or her instructional reading level, which is where pupils have the opportunity to maximise learning without becoming frustrated by the book.
- If the pupil scores 95% or above accuracy and replies correctly to all the questions, he or she should be tested at a higher level.
- If the pupil scores below 90% accuracy, he or she should be tested at a lower level.
- When a pupil is reading at 89% accuracy or below, the book is too difficult and will not only undermine the pupil's confidence but will also have a negative impact on his or her learning.

Reading Record (sample)

Name: Vicki Liu **Date:** 4/5/08 **Age:** 10

Text: Ben Fox Saves the Day **Level:** 6

R.W.: 132 **Accuracy:** 94.7% **S.C. Rate:** 1:4.5

Page			E	SC	Errors MSV	Self-corrections MSV
4	One day, Ben Fox went to the shop (on)	8	1		M S (V)	
	for his mum.	11				
	He was outside the shop (ship|sc)	16		1	M S (V)	(M)(S)V
	getting oranges out of a box, (o-|A)	22	1		M S (V)	
	when the woman from the shop shouted,	29				
	"Stop him! Stop him!"	33				
5	Ben looked up at the woman.	39	1		(M)(S)V	
	"See that boy running away!" she shouted.	46				
	"He has my bag."	50				
6	Ben looked down the street. (s-|A|T)	55	1		M S (V)	
	"I can see a boy.	60				
	He has a blue top and black shorts on	69				
	and he has a red bag," Ben said.	77				
7	"Yes, that is him," said the woman. (that's)	84	1		(M)(S)(V)	
	"And that is my bag!"	89				
	"Stay here," said Ben to the woman.	96				
	"I will get your bag back for you." (I'll)	104	1		(M)(S)(V)	
8	As Ben ran up the street,	110				
	he looked down. (done|R|sc)	113		1	M S (V)	(M)(S)V
	"Oh, no!" he said,	117				
	"I still have my bag of oranges."	124				
	But, he did not have time to stop. (didn't)	132	1		(M)(S)(V)	
Total:			7	2	9	2

Analysis of sample

Level one analysis

Running Words: 132
Errors: 7
Self-corrections: 2
Error Rate: 1:19
Self-correction Rate: 1:4.5
Accuracy: 94.7%

Level one analysis reveals the pupil's error rate, self-correction rate and accuracy rate.

Level two analysis

	Errors			Self-corrections		
	(M)	(S)	(V)	(M)	(S)	(V)
Pupil	4	4	8	2	2	0

Level two analysis looks at the use of information systems. This pupil tends to use more visual cues in their errors; however, he or she is using the meaning and structural cues when self-correcting.

Level three analysis

Level three analysis becomes very important in terms of looking at what the pupil does when reading. The pupil's learning needs can be identified, and this will ultimately structure a teacher's lesson. This pupil displays the following reading behaviours:

- Sometimes re-reads when a mismatch appears
- Tries to predict when unsure
- Seeks help when necessary
- Self-corrects when meaning is disrupted.

Other methods of assessment

For those teachers who require further information, or for those teachers who are not comfortable with taking reading records, a range of assessment sheets have been included:

- Phonics Assessment
- Frequently Used Words Assessment
- Comprehension Assessment

The Phonics Assessment, Frequently Used Words Assessment and Comprehension Assessment must *all* be completed to determine a pupil's instructional reading level.

Phonics Assessment

The Phonics Assessment contains a series of phonological patterns found in the books at that particular reading level.

As these phonic patterns occur frequently throughout the designated reading level, the pupil will need to have a sound knowledge of them in order to read the books successfully.

> The Phonics Assessment can be found in the assessment section in this teacher's guide.

Using the Phonics Assessment

Materials

- 1 teacher's copy of the Phonics Assessment for the *Fast Lane* band
- 1 pupil copy of the Phonics Assessment for the *Fast Lane* band
- 1 copy of the Band Placement Sheet.

Implementation

1. The teacher instructs the pupil to read the words aloud from left to right, *not* from top to bottom.
2. The teacher records the pupil's responses. A correct response is recorded by a tick ✓, an incorrect response is recorded by a cross ✗, and a self-correction is recorded by a cross slash tick ✗/✓. Self-corrections are counted as correct.
3. The teacher counts the number of correct responses in each column and records the number at the bottom of each column.
4. The teacher enters the phonic combinations the pupil needs to focus on in the box "Combinations to focus on" along with any relevant comments.
5. The teacher enters the data collected on the Band Placement Sheet.

Results

A score of 70–80% on the Phonics Assessment, the Frequently Used Words Assessment and the Comprehension Assessment is a good indicator of the pupil's instructional reading level.

Frequently Used Words Assessment

The Frequently Used Words Assessment consists of a selection of words that appear frequently across the books in the designated reading level. Automatic recognition of these words will help pupils to access the texts at both their current level and the next levels.

> The Frequently Used Words Assessment can be found in the assessment section of this teacher's guide.

Using the Frequently Used Words Assessment

Materials

- 1 copy of the Frequently Used Words Assessment for the level
- 1 copy of the Band Placement Sheet for the *Fast Lane* band.

Implementation

1. The teacher instructs the pupil to read the words aloud from left to right, *not* from top to bottom.
2. The teacher records the pupil's responses on the Band Placement Sheet.
   A correct response is recorded by a tick ✓, an incorrect response is recorded by a cross ✗, and a self-correction is recorded by a cross slash tick ✗/✓. Self-corrections are counted as correct.
3. The teacher counts the number of correct responses and adds the number to the total box. The error words are the words the pupil needs to focus on.

Results

A score of 70–80% on the Phonics Assessment, the Frequently Used Words Assessment and the Comprehension Assessment is a good indicator of the pupil's instructional reading level.

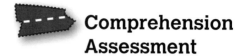

Comprehension Assessment

The Comprehension Assessment is a series of literal, inferential and response questions that pupils will be required to respond to either orally or in writing. The pupils will need access to the book as the questions are not limited to a passage. Some questions refer to visual information found in the texts.

Two Comprehension Assessments are provided for each *Fast Lane* band – one for a fiction and one for a non-fiction book. It is recommended that the teacher assess the pupil using both Comprehension Assessments (but not necessarily at the same time).

> The Comprehension Assessment can be found in the assessment section of this teacher's guide.

Using the Comprehension Assessment

Materials

- 1 copy of the Comprehension Assessment for the *Fast Lane* band
- 1 copy of the fiction book
- 1 copy of the Band Placement Sheet.

Implementation

1. The teacher gives the pupil an orientation to the book. During this orientation time (approximately five minutes), the teacher must give the pupil:
   - the title of the book
   - any proper nouns in the text (e.g. names)
   - any background concepts the pupil needs to access the text (e.g. a brief outline of the content of the text).
2. The pupil reads the book either orally or silently.
3. The pupil completes the questions orally or in writing, as elected by the teacher. The teacher can, if required, read the questions orally for the pupil.
4. The teacher marks the assessment. Literal and inferential questions are marked correct (✓) or incorrect (✗). Response questions are marked Valid or Invalid.
5. The teacher enters the pupil's results on the Band Placement Sheet.

Results

A score of 70–80% on the Phonics Assessment, the Frequently Used Words Assessment and the Comprehension Assessment is a good indicator of the pupil's instructional reading level.

Pro formas

Fast Lane also offers three pro formas to help teachers with graphing and planning.

The pro formas can be found on pages 106–108 of this teacher's guide.

The pro formas are as follows:
- Reading Record *(blank)*
- Reading Graph *(blank)*
- Weekly Individual Literacy Plan *(blank)*

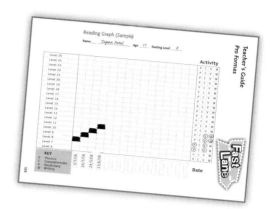

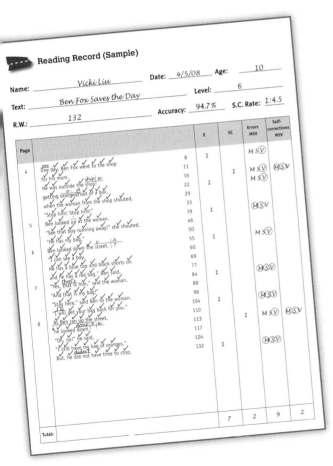

The Reading Graph is designed to record a pupil's progress through the activity sheets for *Fast Lane*. Each time a pupil completes the activities for a level, either the teacher or the pupil fills in the *Reading Graph*. First, the teacher or pupil enters the pupil's name, chronological age and starting level. Secondly, the teacher or pupil fills in:
- the date the activities were completed
- the level
- which activities were done.

As the record of activities is added to the graph, the pupil's progress over time can be gauged.

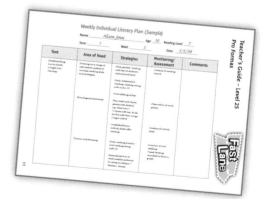

The *Weekly Individual Literacy Plan* is designed to record the teacher's weekly plan for each pupil on *Fast Lane*. The teacher enters the following on the *Weekly Individual Literacy Plan* for each pupil:
- the pupil's name, age and reading level
- the term, week and date
- the book or books the pupil is using
- the pupil's area of need
- strategies for the pupil
- monitoring and assessment to be completed
- any relevant comments.

Fast Lane and primary intervention

Rebecca Tyrrell
Fischer Education Project Ltd

The high-interest, low-readability fiction and non-fiction *Fast Lane* texts have been written for pupils with literacy difficulties and can be used in a range of ways – in guided reading, as a reading intervention scheme in its own right or as a resource to support other literacy interventions (for example, *Catch Up**, *Hi-Five* and *Better Reading Partners*).

Fast Lane supports effective reading intervention programmes in a number of ways.

High interest topics and excellent presentation
Older pupils with reading difficulties are motivated to engage with the texts that cover a range of subject areas of interest to their age group (from computer games, graphic novels, sport, rock music to issues like bullying).

Uses book bands and reading levels
Fast Lane levels are based on the Reading Recovery and PM book bands and reading levels, but are adapted for older pupils – 11-year-olds not 5-year-olds. The subtle colour banding on the spine indicates the level assisting school staff in matching pupils to appropriate book levels. The books come with information on assessment, reading records and guidance on how to move pupils between levels.

Developed for 8 to 14 year olds
With limited resources traditionally available for this age group, *Fast Lane* can also provide continuity across the transition between primary and secondary schools (Key Stages 2–3 or P7–P8)

Facilitates assessment for learning
The assessments provided can be used to identify where the pupils are in their learning and where they need to go next (including guidance on running records, phonic assessment, high frequency words and comprehension).

More words per page and per text
The increased word count (that rises with each level) provides pupils with opportunities to build reading fluency, speed and stamina, which is not possible with shorter more restricted texts.

Controlled vocabulary development *(1 new word for 16 familiar words)*
The controlled vocabulary development ensures the books remain accessible. New words (particularly subject-based, technical vocabulary) are deliberately repeated several times in order to provide opportunities for practice and learning. This structured approach facilitates the clarification process during the book introduction and in the return to the text.

Age-appropriate language structures
Although the 'reading age' of the books may be several years below the chronological age of the pupils due to their literacy levels, language structures should reflect each pupil's age. Thus *Fast Lane* books include longer, more complex structures, incorporating the use of connectives that will be needed for reinforcing features of text type and provide models and support for both oral and written work.

Equal provision of non-fiction and fiction texts
It has been estimated that 93% of the curriculum requires pupils to read or understand non-fiction texts! *Fast Lane* enables pupils to access non-fiction texts at their level in preparation for the sort of text they will be encountering in class in other curriculum subjects. This is particularly important as language use in non-fiction is often different from fiction.

Strong curriculum links
Subject-related texts enable links to be made between areas being targeted in the intervention (clarifying subject related vocabulary and concepts) and teaching taking place in the classroom – which is key to the transfer of relevant skills to the classroom.

Clear text types
Unfamiliarity with the features of different text types can have a negative impact on comprehension. Texts based on clear text types enable explicit teaching of specific text type features so that pupils become familiar with them in their reading – drawing evidence from the texts during book introductions and in the return to the text. The pupils can then begin to use other text types more confidently in their writing, and will be better equipped to read them when they encounter them in other subject classes.

---

*CATCH UP LITERACY: Catch Up Literacy is a structured intervention for learners who find reading difficult. It has been proven to be an effective tool which can significantly help struggling readers in just 10–15 minutes a week. For further information, visit www.catchup.org.uk

Layout features

The texts exemplify the components of real texts which the pupils will encounter in the classroom, the library and at home. For example, in fiction the use of chapters, chapter headings, illustrations and paragraphs; in non-fiction, the use of a wide variety of features, such as bold print, text boxes, charts, maps, diagrams, labels, indexes, glossaries and cross-sectional diagrams. As a result, pupils can learn how to 'read' and draw meaning from different information sources.

Using the mini audio CD

The mini audio CD provides motivational value when pupils follow up their reading, enabling them to listen to the entire text, and also providing a model for fluency and phrasing. It also provides the option for pupils with language difficulties or English as a second language, to hear the text before working with it in a more structured way.

Reading guidance notes and activities accompany each text

The notes in the back of every *Fast Lane* reading book provide a framework for conducting a full guided reading or Wave 3 intervention lesson. They indicate aspects to address before, during and after reading. For example, pointers are given for the start of the lesson that involve activating background knowledge, clarifying new vocabulary/grammatical structures, drawing attention to the features of text type and layout and opportunities for teaching word level/phonic skills at the beginning of the lesson. Later guidance is suggested for developing a deeper understanding of the text.

Follow-up activities

Downloadable activity sheets are provided on the free CD-ROM which accompanies each teacher's guide. On the completion of a reading session, the teacher may have observed the pupil struggling with one of the three key areas of reading: comprehension (meaning), vocabulary (language structure) or phonics (visual). They can then choose the appropriate activity sheet in order to practice or reinforce this literacy skill.

Case study: using *Fast Lane* with Hi-Five

The Fischer Education Project 'Hi-Five' is a Wave 3 reading and writing intervention programme, focusing mainly on non-fiction texts for groups of up to three pupils (at Year 5/P6 and beyond) working at a low level National Curriiculum level 2. Hi-Five's programme begins at approximately *Fast Lane* Orange band (or level 15) and lasts for at least ten weeks. However, pupils with a limited oral language may need to work at a level lower for non-fiction than for fiction.

The highly supportive assessments provided help ensure a strong match of book to pupil. As well as aiming to develop independent reading and writing strategies, Hi-Five targets study skills (prediction, clarification, questioning, summarising), speaking and comprehension, and targets different text type features. There is a four-lesson structure with two reading days and two writing/editing days centred around one text. *Fast Lane* has proven ideal for those pupils who have been working with the text books provided for the first few weeks and are now ready for longer and more challenging texts at a similar or higher level.

The length of the *Fast Lane* books requires more reading stamina, whilst still introducing new words at a rate appropriate for an instructional text. The complex sentence structures provide good models for both oral and written work and the levelling ensures texts can be correctly matched to pupil ability. The teacher's notes within each book provide guidance for the book introduction (triggering background knowledge and highlighting text type features, vocabulary and word work) and there are examples of different levels of questioning. The mini audio CD encourages fluency and strengthens comprehension while providing model language structures that will enhance writing and the teacher's notes include ideas for text based writing focuses. The class based worksheets, that offer practice for areas of difficulty, provide a key link between the intervention and the classroom.

Fast Lane matching chart

Fast Lane band/ level*	England & Wales National Curriculum level**	Key borderline skills for assessment
Yellow 6	Secure level 1 (1B)	
Yellow 7	Secure level 1 (1B)	
Yellow 8	Secure level 1 (1B)	
Blue 9	Secure level 1 (1B)	
Blue 10	Secure level 1 (1B)	
Blue 11	Secure level 1 (1B)	
Green 12	High level 1 (1A)	**Moving to level 2:** 1) comprehends text with less reliance on illustrations; 2) Uses punctuation and text to read with expression and fluency; 3) Recalls some straightforward information from text (e.g. character names, ingredients); 4) Sometimes makes simple inference from text (e.g. how character feels); 5) Identifies basic organisation (beginning, end), some types of punctuation.
Green 13	High level 1 (1A)	
Green 14	High level 1 (1A)	
Orange 15	High level 1 (1A)	
Orange 16	High level 2 (1A)	
Turquoise 17	Low level 2 (2C)	**Secure level 2:** 1) key words are read on sight and strategies are used to decode unfamiliar words; 2) some account is taken of punctuation for fluency and expression; 3) strategies are used to recall the most basic information from the text; 4) prompts from the text are used to make the most simple inferences; 5) there is a basic awareness of how texts are organised (e.g. beginning and ending of a story); 6) successful language choices are identified; 7) there is some recognition that the writer has a purpose and viewpoint, expressed as simple likes and dislikes; 8) there is a recognition that different texts have different features. **Moving to level 3:** 1) underline key words in questions; 2) look back and use information in texts to answer questions; 3) scan text quickly to find key words; 4) begin to speculate on the inferred meaning of key words and phrases; 5) use organisational features of non-fiction to find info quickly.
Turquoise 18	Low level 2 (2C)	
Purple 19	Low level 2 (2C)	
Purple 20	Low level 2 (2C)	
Gold 21	Secure level 2 (2B)	
Gold 22	Secure level 2 (2B)	
Silver 23	High level 2/low level 3 (2A/3C)	
Silver 24	High level 2/low level 3 (2A/3C)	**Secure level 3:** 1) identifies the most obvious points in a text; 2) selects text (not always entirely relevantly) to justify comments; 3) establishes meaning at a literal level with some (occasionally inaccurate) speculation about inferred meaning; 4) simpler features of organisation at text level can be identified; 5) features of language can be identified, without comment on effect; 6) the writer's main purpose and viewpoint is identified but does not speculate on the impact on the reader. **Moving to level 4:** 1) Select text appropriately to use in quotations and for note making; 2) carry out independent research using more than one source; 3) begin to make inferences in a way that is increasingly rooted in the text; 4) identify the main features of text organisation with an appreciation of their function; 5) comment on the writer's choice of language and its effect; 6) begin to comment on writer's purpose and the effect on the reader.
Emerald 25	Secure level 3 (3B)	

* FAST LANE AND CATCH UP LITERACY LEVELS: Catch Up Literacy Levels support the professional judgements of teachers, teaching assistants and carers when they are selecting books for struggling readers. Books are graded into 12 levels of text difficulty and grouped by age and interest level. We are currently working with Catch Up to grade Fast Lane books into Catch Up Literacy Levels. See www.catchup.org.uk.
** National Curriculum levels are used as the basis for Fischer Hi-five and Reading Challenge

Fast Lane and secondary intervention

Hayley Davies-Edwards
Senior Curriculum Development Adviser (English), Wokingham Borough Council

Organising intervention programmes

Pupils entering secondary school with below average literacy abilities (for example, National Curriculum level 3 or below) will usually need additional support with reading and writing. Most schools choose to carry out baseline testing of these pupils, thus enabling them to establish a sub-level or reading age which can be used to judge progress made during the course of Year 7, as well as the impact of any intervention programmes.

The organisation of reading intervention or catch-up programmes varies from school to school, but examples of good practice would include:

- 30 minutes of one-to-one support twice a week for 10 weeks (on a programme such as *Reading Challenge*) in a before-school, lunchtime or after-school session. Some schools choose to provide this support on a withdrawal basis.
- In-class one-to-one support from a teaching assistant, to enable the pupil to apply the learning in the additional reading intervention sessions.
- In-class or withdrawal support in the form of small group or 'guided' sessions for pupils with a similar learning need.
- Whole-class intervention for pupils delivered by the teacher with teaching assistant support (particularly those targeting NC level 3 or level 4).

Using *Fast Lane* as a secondary intervention scheme

Fast Lane would be very successful if run as a scheme on its own, as it addresses features at sentence and word level which can be neglected in existing programmes. Examples of this are understanding the use of complex sentences, contractions, cohesion devices, time adverbials and chronological connectives. *Fast Lane* provides teachers with opportunities to highlight these features and discuss their role in communicating meaning.

The range of texts in *Fast Lane* is extremely varied and encompasses all of the main text types which a pupil would encounter in the secondary curriculum.

For the disengaged reader, there is an opportunity to interact with characters and themes which are suited to the age and interests of early teenagers and this, coupled with the dynamic graphics and illustrations is a powerful tool for encouraging pupil engagement.

In addition, the books do not have the 'childish' presentational features of some reading texts for struggling readers, but are presented in a more grown-up way, sometimes using photographs and sometimes a teenage comic-strip or graphic novel style, which is popular amongst young teens.

Finally, the non-fiction books can be linked to the new National Curriculum subjects, such as Science, Design and technology, Citizenship and History. Details of this are found inside the readers and in the book-by-book section of this guide (see pages 34–51).

Using *Fast Lane's* reading notes and assessment and activity sheets

Fast Lane's downloadable activity sheets (found on the CD-ROM at the front of each Teacher's Guide) link directly to assessment focuses:

- Comprehension (meaning) activity sheets offer practice for information retrieval, a key skill for AF2. Some of the questions require inference, which is a crucial AF3 skill area for moving to level 4.
- The vocabulary activities enable a consolidation of skills of decoding at AF1, particularly where pupils are weaker at using a range of strategies to work out the meaning of a word. This will be of particular benefit in working with pupils who enter the secondary phase at level 2 or below.
- The phonics activity sheets support the development of AF1, where pupils are unsure about phoneme/grapheme relationships. This will be of particular use for those pupils who enter secondary school with a reading level below level 2.
- Some of the writing activities in 'After reading' (in the reader notes) encourage pupils to summarise the purpose of texts (AF6), which is a particular weakness with pupils working below level 4.

- The 'free' nature of the personal response writing activities in the reader notes can be used to meet a range of AFs and this varies from focusing on the language of the text (AF5) to making simple observations about structure and organisation (AF4).
- The assessment sheets are very impressive in that they break progression in reading down into small and very measurable steps. Instructions on how to assess and re-assess are clear and unambiguous. The pro formas allow for detailed records of a pupil's progression to be kept and this will help both formative decisions about next learning steps and also summative reporting to parents.

Using *Fast Lane* alongside other secondary intervention schemes

There are a number of one-to-one and small group intervention schemes available for teachers in secondary schools, and *Fast Lane* can be used to complement these.

Reading Challenge

Fast Lane can be used alongside the *Reading Challenge* intervention programme, which targets level 4 in reading, notable where pupils have either 'Book knowledge'; 'Reading for meaning' or 'Reading strategies' as their 'Top Challenge'. *Fast Lane* supports the development of inference and the more independent use of active reading strategies to explore meaning and make a more critical response to texts. *Reading Challenge* can be blended with *Fast Lane* for pupils targeting level 4, due to the nature of the comprehension questions in the *Fast Lane* reading notes (or found in the CD-ROM activity sheets), which move from literal to inferential, a key competency for reading at level 4.

Targeting level 4 in reading

Schools which use the 12 *Targeting level 4 in reading* whole-class lessons (from the National Strategy) will find that *Fast Lane* supports scanning for information; reading different ways of presenting information; making sense of difficult texts; summarising; reading for meaning; exploring character, setting and mood and exploring language choices and author attitudes. Additionally, pupils targeting level 4 would benefit from reading a range of fiction and non-fiction *Fast Lane* texts at levels 23–25.

Assessing Pupil Progress and the Framework for teaching English

The Assessing Pupil Progress materials are used to establish curricular targets for pupils who are struggling with the inferential aspects of reading at level 4.

- *Fast Lane* guidance notes and comprehension activity sheets also distinguish between the literal, inferential and response aspects of reading. The English National Curriculum **sees these on a continuum** within Assessment Focus 3, with personal response being lower on the continuum than inference. As pupils move from personal response to inference, they are developing a level 4 skill: *"In responding to a range of texts, pupils show understanding of significant ideas, themes, events and characters, beginning to use inference and deduction."* (NC level 4 description).
- *Fast Lane* guidance notes focus closely on the features of text type (and a wide range of text types are provided in the scheme). This is ideal for teaching the conventions and features of text types, as outlined in the new *Framework for Teaching English*, which enables teachers to identify learning objectives for Years 7–11 on a **sliding continuum of progression**.
- Pupils also receive support with developing a P.E.E. (Point, Evidence, Explanation) reading response, which is a feature of reading assessment at Key Stage 3.
- The table on page 31 shows how Fast Lane can be linked up with the National Strategy assessment focuses.

Literacy progress units

Literacy Progress Units are used for boosting struggling readers in Year 7: *Phonics; Information retrieval and Reading between the lines*. *Fast Lane* can be used to augment these schemes, as the 'Before', 'During', and 'After reading' activities support pupils' exploration of text type, visual literacy, phonological awareness; vocabulary in context; the development of inferential meaning; fluency and punctuation patterns; linking the visual and written and following up with a range of targeted activities at word, sentence and text level. This provides a very appropriate follow-up for pupils who have completed one or more of the *Literacy Progress Units*.

Using Assessment Focuses with *Fast Lane*

Assessment Focus	Using the reader guidance notes (inside reader cover) and CD-ROM activity sheets
AF1 – use a range of strategies, including accurate decoding of text, to read for meaning	*Vocabulary (structure) activities* encourage pupils to use a range of strategies to read words and work out their meaning.
AF2 – understand, describe, select or retrieve information, events or ideas from texts and use quotation and reference to text	*Comprehension (meaning) activities* focus on information retrieval and allow pupils to practise these in a range of ways.
AF3 – deduce, infer or interpret information, events or ideas from texts	*During reading guidance* supports focus on moving pupils to increasingly secure use of inference, which for level 4 must be securely rooted in the text. *Comprehension activities* include focus on developing inference.
AF4 – identify and comment on the structure and organisation of texts, including grammatical and presentational features at text level	*During reading guidance* enables a focus on the features of the text type at text level. Guidance given allows for an exploration of the components of both narrative and non-fiction text types.
AF5 – explain and comment on writers' use of language, including grammatical and literary features at word and sentence level	*During reading guidance* enables a focus on the features of the text type at word and sentence level. It may focus on the use of nouns, adverbs, adjectives and verbs, and explore conjunctions, subordinate clauses and specific features of punctuation, such as ellipses and quotation marks.
AF6 – identify and comment on writers' purposes and viewpoints, and the overall effect of the text on the reader	*Before* and *During reading guidance* encourages pupils to speculate about why a text has been written.
AF7 – relate texts to their social, cultural and historical traditions	*During reading guidance* encourages pupils to think about the relationship between the words chosen and the context of the text.

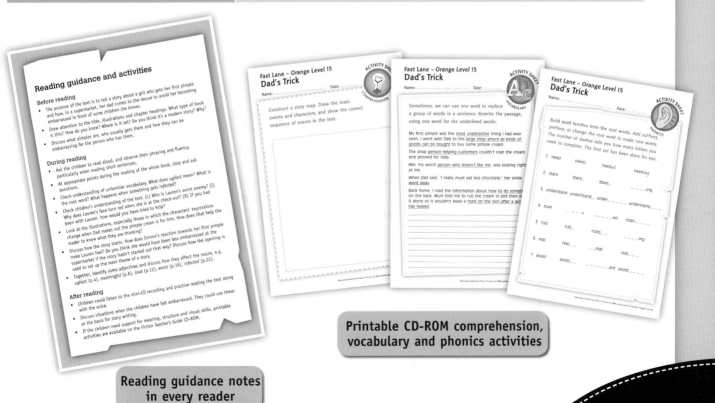

Reading guidance notes in every reader

Printable CD-ROM comprehension, vocabulary and phonics activities

31

Fast Lane and other Curricula

Fast Lane and Scotland

In Scottish schools, there is no doubt that pupils who have reading difficulties, or are disengaged learners, need appropriate support and at times a great deal of encouragement in order to progress the reading skills they need for life. This also applies to pupils who have English as a second language.

Reading and learning opportunities need to meet the variety of needs each individual has, so programmes need to be rich and varied, offering success for the reader. Pupils learning to read, especially those with specific learning needs, require texts that:

1. are structured
2. are consistent in style and language
3. can be read at an appropriate pace
4. include a variety of contexts and genres
5. have high interest content.

In this way they can experience the breadth and width of reading opportunities that hold the key to success.

Fast Lane is a programme worthy of very close consideration for inclusion in any reading support programme in school. In Scottish schools, it would be highly suitable for the top end of primary and early secondary (Scottish P6–P9), and if used in this way would provide continuity of experience at transition time.

The books are arranged in graded reading levels and bands and provide a wide range of reading experiences for the pupils. The books are attractive to the reader, well laid out and offer, from the early levels onwards, increasing vocabulary and challenge. The books are short, thus offering success for the reader as a confidence boost. Illustrations in the fiction books are bright and eye-catching and support the reader to decode the information on each page. The non-fiction books are beautifully illustrated and the variety of illustration styles provides purposeful practice for the reader in the use of appropriate illustrative genres. As the reader progresses through the levels of *Fast Lane*, both fiction and non-fiction books have increased written text. Usefully, all non-fiction titles include a contents, index and glossary.

Each book includes an audio CD that enhances pupil experience. The reader may be able to work independently and benefit from reading the book, supported by playing the audio CD whilst reading. At each level there are activity sheets to further develop literacy skills. These sheets provide assessment information which, coupled with teacher assessment, indicate next steps for the reader. There are a number of books at each level that provide breadth of experience, but a reader who is making good progress may move to the next level without necessarily completing the level they are working on. Through the titles at each level the reader will encounter a variety of purpose and genres. Whether the focus is reporting, recounting, explaining or describing – skills needed in other areas of the Scottish curriculum – the reader will enhance their experience of reading through exposure to this range of essential reading skills.

It is encouraging that *Fast Lane* provides an extensive selection of highly motivating, graded reads. This in itself is advantageous to readers, teachers and supporters alike. However, without additional structure this may not be enough. A reader's motivation can be short lived if there are not routine, additional support mechanisms or a real feeling of success and progress. For these reasons *Fast Lane* provides a variety of additional components. As previously mentioned audio support can augment the readers' experience, guiding them at an appropriate pace in a paired reading type situation. Teaching notes are available for each book to guide the teacher (or teaching assistant), giving practical advice on what to do, before, during and after reading. Three activity sheets accompany each book that provide readers with extended experiences and the teacher with close assessment information. The activity sheets concentrate on comprehension, vocabulary and phonics.

Assessment sheets provide opportunities for recording progress in phonics, comprehension and retention of high frequency words. Pro formas are available which support the teacher in recording information, mapping progress and individual planning for each reader. As well as *Fast Lane's* wide variety of texts, designed for struggling readers, there are rigorous assessment opportunities that link strongly to the Curriculum for Excellence's emphasis on personalisation and the close assessment and tracking of pupils' learning.

"Competence and confidence in literacy, including competence in grammar, spelling and the spoken word, are essential for progress in all areas of the curriculum ... Every teacher in each area of the curriculum needs to find opportunities to encourage young people to explain their thinking, debate their ideas and read and write at a level which will help them to develop their language skills further."

A Curriculum for Excellence, Learning and teaching languages

I have no doubt that *Fast Lane* meets the criteria and expectations of the 5–14 curriculum in Scotland through the range of experiences provided. Furthermore, guidance for The Curriculum for Excellence (ACfE) highlights the need for more integrated teaching approaches between the curriculum subjects. *Fast Lane* provides this by providing a range of fascinating themes and topics linked to other curriculum subjects: Science, History, Geography and Citizenship, in particular.

If we are to inspire effective learning, then we need effective programmes such as *Fast Lane* to raise the confidence of individuals, particularly those who are struggling to achieve levels A and B in our language curriculum. Reading and writing are the key tools to unlock the whole curriculum for learners and a programme such as *Fast Lane* can support learners who find those subjects most challenging.

Iain Campbell
Headteacher St Margaret's Primary School, Falkirk

Fast Lane and Northern Ireland

The *Fast Lane* series can be used to support pupils' achievement of the levels of progression in the Language and Literacy strand of the Northern Ireland Curriculum (Primary). In addition to offering progressively levelled reading books, the guidance activities in the back of the readers suggest opportunities for talking and listening/writing strands.

Fast Lane levels	Scottish 5–14 levels					Northern Ireland levels of progression (reading)
	Reading for information	Reading for enjoyment	Reflect on the writer's craft	Awareness of genre	Knowledge of language	
Yellow levels 6–8	A/B	A/B	A/B	A/B	A/B	Level 1
Blue levels 9–11	A/B	A/B	A/B	A/B	A/B	Towards level 2
Green levels 12–14	A/B	A/B	A/B	A/B	A/B	Towards level 2
Orange levels 15–16	B	B	B	B	B	Level 2
Turquoise levels 17–18	B	B	B	B	B	Level 2
Purple levels 19–20	B/C	B/C	B/C	B/C	B/C	Level 2
Gold levels 21–22	B/C	B/C	B/C	B/C	B/C	Level 2
Silver levels 23–24	C	C	C	C	C	Towards level 3
Emerald level 25	C	C	C	C	C	Towards level 3

Fast Lane Fiction titles (Yellow to Emerald/levels 6 to 25)

Fast Lane band	Level	Book and author	Text type	Curriculum links	Word count
Yellow	6	BEN FOX SAVES THE DAY Carmel Reilly	Story with a familiar setting	Citizenship	349
	6	DAD AND DAN GO FISHING Nicolas Brasch	Story with a familiar setting	n/a	280
	6	NOISES IN THE NIGHT Carmel Reilly	Story with a familiar setting	n/a	334
	7	HARRY HELPS OUT Carmel Reilly	Story with a familiar setting	n/a	352
	7	THE MESS Michael Wagner	Story with a familiar setting	n/a	304
	7	A NIGHT OUT Carmel Reilly	Story with a familiar setting	n/a	338
	8	TAKING OFF Carmel Reilly	Story with a familiar setting	Citizenship	385
	8	JEWELLERY SHOP ROBBERY Carmel Reilly	Story with a familiar setting	Citizenship	353
	8	THE MYSTERY OF THE MISSING BIKE Nicolas Brasch	Mystery story	Science	327

Words in context	Frequently used words	Phonic opportunities	Related activity and assessment sheets
blue, idea, oranges, past, rolled, running, shouted, woman	boy, children, down, getting, him, ran, said, stop, that, went	Graphemes rk and ck	CD: Meaning, structure and visual activities
catch, cooked, excited, funny, last, laughed, seaweed, stopped	Dad, eat, got, home, looked, mum, of, said, was, with	CVC words and phoneme /ea/	CD: Meaning, structure and visual activities
asleep, dinner, friend, hearing-aid, helped, jumped, noise, stayed, window	all, but, her, looked, night, said, stay, that, was, yes	Phonemes /oo/ and /ee/	CD: Meaning, structure and visual activities
anything, computer, next door, past, sitting, something, sometimes, stopped, told, works	have, her, Mrs, out, said, she, want, with, you	Adjacent consonant 'nk', phoneme /oo/	CD: Meaning, structure and visual activities
broom, clean, cupboard, empty, friends, hard, idea, leaned, mess, more, sweep	all, good, have, not, now, most, out, said, was, went, you	Phonemes /or/ and /air/	CD: Meaning, structure and visual activities
alone, bumped, dancing, grabbed, hall, laughing, middle, shook, shouting, started, think	have, into, looked, not, over, said, she, they, were, you	Phonemes /oo/ and /e/	CD: Meaning, structure and visual activities
behind, can't, cool, don't, hill, I'm, it's, jobs, kids, money, paint, raced, shout, skateboard	all, around, for, friend, look, most, out, said, she, take, up, was, you	Phonemes /ow/ and /ai/	CD: Meaning, structure and visual activities
black, detective, door, house, jewellery, noise, police, red, reporter, robbery, two	around, again, could, his, inside, next, said, saw, she, there, that, was, what	Phonemes /k/ and /ee/	CD: Meaning, structure and visual activities
bike, detective, driveway, followed, garden, marks, missing, mystery, notebook, pen, remember, solved	could, down, did, find, for, front, have, said, saw, them, there, were, your, you	Phonemes /ow/ and /k/ and /oo/	CD: Meaning, structure and visual activities

Fast Lane band	Level	Book and author	Text type	Curriculum links	Word count
Blue	9	ON THE TEAM Peter Millett	Story with a familiar setting	Citizenship	330
	9	MAGIC TRICKS Carmel Reilly	Story with a familiar setting	Citizenship	394
	9	TIME TRAVEL: DINOSAURS Nicolas Brasch	Fantasy story	n/a	445
	10	DAD AND DAN GO CAMPING Nicolas Brasch	Story with a familiar setting	n/a	354
	10	BUZZ AND ZIP GET LOST Carmel Reilly	Story set in an imaginary world	n/a	383
	10	SHARK! Peter Millett	Adventure story	n/a	347
	11	SAYING GOODBYE Carmel Reilly	Story dealing with issues	Citizenship	370
	11	THE CHALK CIRCLE Nicolas Brasch	Story dealing with issues	Citizenship	385
	11	JUMP! Peter Millett	Adventure story	Physical Education	356

Words in context	Frequently used words	Phonic opportunities	Related activity and assessment sheets
basketball, game, hoop, pass, ran, Saturday, school, shoot, steal, team, winners	did, good, like, me, really, said, so, then, was, you	Grapheme ll and word ending ed	CD: Meaning, structure and visual activities
cape, flowers, hat, laughed, magic, rabbit, rings, school, shocked, show, stage, table, tricks	another, but, called, could, day, going, he, his, last, of, on, out, put, was	Phonemes /j/ and /s/	CD: Meaning, structure and visual activities
brother, button, dinosaur, floor, garden, jungle, lunch, reptile, tree, trunk	all, are, come, from, here, lot, over	Unstressed vowels and adjacent consonants 'tr'	CD: Meaning, structure and visual activities
camping, gear, grabbed, middle, packed, pizza, remember, scratched, unpacked	always, into, out, said, soon, that, were, when, would	Adjacent consonants mp and lk	CD: Meaning, structure and visual activities
grabbed, hundreds, monster, nothing, odd, planet, spaceship, terrible, ugliest, zoom	could, have, more, out, put, want, was, what, where, very	Phoneme /oo/ and adjacent consonants ck	CD: Meaning, structure and visual activities
bumped, dolphin, face, paddled, popped, shadow, stared, surfboard	down, gone, just, their, they, under, was, you	Phonemes /f/ and /sh/	CD: Meaning, structure and visual activities
believe, dressed up, freckled, goodbye, handed, odd, prizes, radio, remember	from, gone, Grandpa, just, much, put, said, that, today	Phonemes /oo/ and /ee/	CD: Meaning, structure and visual activities
bench, chalk, cool, earphone, empty, Mp3 player, owner, power	gone, off, saw, some, then, they, took, was, were	Phonemes /ee/ and /ch/	CD: Meaning, structure and visual activities
blind, breath, bumped, cord, dipped, emergency, excited, fear, guide dog, instructor, parachute, problem	about, came, come, have, here, moved, out, this, your	Phonemes /ear/ and /ai/	CD: Meaning, structure and visual activities

Fast Lane band	Level	Book and author	Text type	Curriculum links	Word count
Green	12	THE CALL OF THE WOLF Carmel Reilly	Adventure story	Citizenship	420
Green	12	THE GAME Peter Millett	Fantasy story	ICT	501
Green	12	SUPER FIT Peter Millett	Story with a familiar setting	Physical Education	441
Green	13	DON'T EMBARRASS ME, DAD Sharon Holt	Story with issues	Citizenship	506
Green	13	METAL MOUTH Julie Mitchell	Fantasy story	Science	466
Green	13	TIME TRAVEL: SHIP AHOY Nicolas Brasch	Science fiction fantasy story	History	460
Green	14	BUZZ TAKES OVER Carmel Reilly	Story set in an imaginary world	n/a	474
Green	14	SECRET AGENT Carmel Reilly	Mystery story	Design and Technology	469
Green	14	THE INVENTORS' CLUB Nicholas Brasch	Story with a familiar setting	Design and Technology and Science	436

Words in context	Frequently used words	Phonic opportunities	Related activity and assessment sheets
cave, darkness, fire, gulp, heard, howl, hungry, knife, listened, shadow, shiver, sticks, test, warming, wolf, woods	almost, alone, father, few, gave, important, knew, know, past, small, suddenly, walk, would	Phonemes /or/ and /oa/ and /ear/	CD: Meaning, structure and visual activities
air, blasted, computer, control tower, cyborg, disk, earphones, flashing, game, giant, keyboard, laser, noise, panel, screen, voice	happening, jammed, know, quickly, spun, swooped, through, upside, whispered	Phonemes /igh/ and /ow/ and /k/	CD: Meaning, structure and visual activities
coach, dinner, fingers, fit, gym, indoor rock climbing, library, plaster, project, science, surprised, teacher, training, volleyball	afternoon, again, almost, better, guess, hardly, know, move, right, shame, suddenly, tomorrow	Phonemes /ai/ and /ee/	CD: Meaning, structure and visual activities
basketball, burgers, coach, dribble, fouls, friends, chips, game, homework, practice, rubbish, rules, sister, sleep over, team, whistle	after, because, breath, easy, embarrass, forgets, forward, guess, live, Saturday, thinking, tomorrow, watch, why, worry, would, wrong	Phonemes /ee/ and /oa/ and /igh/	CD: Meaning, structure and visual activities
braces, dentist, dinner, food, fork, hair, jewellery, lightning, magnet, metal, mouth, news, school, science	afternoon, all right, ate, becoming, felt, full, later, life, matter, okay, playing, problem, sorry, talk, terrible, worry	Phonemes /ee/ and /ai/ and /igh/	CD: Meaning, structure and visual activities
adventure, America, birthday, Charlie, crowd, dock, England, Georgia, iceberg, passenger ship, port, time machine, Titanic, water	about, afraid, clear, could, died, different, held, inside, little, okay, pulled, snapped, standing, suddenly, taking, thank, tried, wait	Phonemes /ee/ and /ai/ and /igh/	CD: Meaning, structure and visual activities
auto-pilot, black hole, computer, controls, galaxy, pirates, pods	around, door, going, right, said, were, what, your	Phoneme /ee/ and Grapheme ed	CD: Meaning, structure and visual activities
agent, blast, enemy, mask, trackers, traffic, untied, warehouse	fast, full, gone, great, inside, somewhere, there, under, you're	Phoneme /air/ and Grapheme ow	CD: Meaning, structure and visual activities
bounce, hanging, invention, inventors, pretend, seconds, secret, springs, squeezed, third	could, every, from, show, something, their, they, were, what	Phonemes /ur/ and /ow/	CD: Meaning, structure and visual activities

39

Fast Lane band	Level	Book and author	Text type	Curriculum links	Word count
Orange	15	EVERYTHING IS CHANGING Carmel Reilly	Historical fiction	History	532
Orange	15	THE GOLDEN TOUCH Nicolas Brasch	Greek myth	History	525
Orange	15	DAD'S TRICK Julia Wall	Story in a familiar setting	Science and Citizenship	536
Orange	15	MARTY AND THE MAGAZINE Julia Wall	Story with an issue	Citizenship	558
Orange	16	NEW TRICKS Carmel Reilly	Story with a familiar setting	PHSE	519
Orange	16	MERCURY AND THE WOODCUTTER Peter Millett	Traditional fable	History	568
Orange	16	WAIT AND SEE Julia Wall	Story with a familiar setting	Citizenship	501
Orange	16	SCARY MOVIE Peter Millett	Story with a familiar setting	Citizenship and Science	507

Words in context	Frequently used words	Phonic opportunities	Related activity and assessment sheets
boss, changing, garage, important, lemonade, movies, oven, run-down, track	ever, everything, first, gave, hours, house, keep, next, such, what	Phonemes /t/ and /ur/	CD: Meaning, structure and visual activities
appeared, downfall, fantastic, feast, granted, grateful, kindness, palace, pity, power, rewarded, shelter, shock, starve	asked, asleep, knew, money, over, some, such, through, too, warm	Phoneme /igh/ and grapheme ng	CD: Meaning, structure and visual activities
assistant, disappeared, enemy, infected, instructions, meaningful, scar, supermarket, ugliest, understood	after, first, front, own, right, seen, some, thought, under	Grapheme ea and phoneme /u/	CD: Meaning, structure and visual activities
believed, chose, hearty, magazines, matter, nodded, pizza, reviews, shaking, slipped	after, been, behind, fast, liked, most, music, there, thing, turn	Phoneme /z/ and grapheme ye	CD: Meaning, structure and visual activities
assistant, audience, cheered, comedy, imagine, magician, Natalie, pale, perform, practise, practising, puzzles, sawing, shoes, tricks, wrong	careful, disappear, fine, laugh, nervous, numbers, really, remember, swap, usual, which, wonderful	Phonemes /ee/ and /ur/	CD: Meaning, structure and visual activities
axe, dishonest, firewood, golden, handle, honest, Mercury, riverbank, silver, slid, strength, woodcutter, wooden	angrily, beautiful, chopped, ground, lucky, near, rest, sharp, sobbed, splash, stared, wiped, wonderful	Phonemes /oo/ and /e/	CD: Meaning, structure and visual activities
arguing, blond, colour, deal, dye, gel, hairdresser, hallway, heads, hedgehog, ideas, instead, minds, person, similar, tails, toss, won	alike, apart, guess, hoped, laughed, other, stared, surprised, wait, wondered	Phonemes /ai/ and /f/	CD: Meaning, structure and visual activities
argh, couch, crawling, curling, DVD, escaped, glass, hairy, hurt, inch, movie, remote control, scary, scooped, spider, wriggled	between, carefully, dropped, friendly, gasped, grateful, nearly, other, silently, smiled, stared	Phonemes /ee/ and /er/	CD: Meaning, structure and visual activities

Fast Lane band	Level	Book and author	Text type	Curriculum links	Word count
Turquoise	17	BATTLE OF THE BANDS Peter Millett	Story with a familiar setting	n/a	631
	17	GADGET BOY SAVES THE DAY George Ivanoff	Story set in an imaginary world	n/a	610
	17	INSIDE THE GATE Carmel Reilly	Story from a different culture	n/a	652
	17	RENOVATIONS Carmel Reilly	Fantasy story	n/a	525
	18	GLACIER Mike Graf	Adventure story	Geography and Science	586
	18	THE GRAVEYARD SHIFT Carmel Reilly	Story with a familiar setting	Citizenship	637
	18	THE BULLY Julie Mitchell	Story with issues	PSHE	603
	18	THE INVENTOR'S CLUB MEETS AGAIN Nicolas Brasch	Story with a familiar setting	Design and Technology	605

Words in context	Frequently used words	Phonic opportunities	Related activity and assessment sheets
awesome, bands, battle, beat, blankly, butterflies, competition, curtain, drummer, drumsticks, electric, envelope, guitar, hugged, hush, microphone, perform, plugged, silent, smart, song, speakers, strummed, wedding, wild	another, forever, front, giving, knew, know, loudly, opened, their, there's, they're, turn, whispered, without, yeah, yelled	Phonemes /air/ and /k/	CD: Meaning, structure and visual activities
basement, bedroom, buildings, cage, Candyman, captured, city, decay, flash, gadgets, hero, inventor, invisibility, jet-pack, lolly, Metro, newspaper, reports, sugar, supply, toffee, tooth, traffic, villains, visible	chance, choose, covered, full, giant, heard, just, main, open, own, special, towards, turned, use, where	Phonemes /j/ and /k/	CD: Meaning, structure and visual activities
bananas, dirt, doorstep, dusty, farms, fruit, gate, Grandma, grew, leave, market, nursery, pile, plant, shade, speak, tired, town, trees, vegetable, whipping, wind	asks, covered, follow, green, huge, inside, large, own, say, shouldn't, speak, sure, welcome, women	Phoneme /oo/	CD: Meaning, structure and visual activities
bang, bedroom, breakfast, bricks, build, busy, downstairs, dust, easy, frowned, genie, grumpy, owner, puzzled, renovation, serious, shrugged, toppling, tricks, upstairs, weakly, wearing	because, could, grumpily, huge, knew, mean, might, noise, realised, too, towards, would, yourself	Phonemes /ar/ and /e/	CD: Meaning, structure and visual activities
bounce, crampons, crevasse, glacier, gripped, hiking, ice axe, ledge, planted, polished	carefully, each, hear, looked, over, pulled, rock, shouted, they, too, very, we'll	Phonemes /ai/ and /oa/ and /or/	CD: Meaning, structure and visual activities
cemetery, howling, nonsense, normal, peered, searching, skeleton, spirit, spooky, stand-up, surprised, zombies	great, heard, house, kind, know, laugh, really, through, walked, work	Phoneme /s/	CD: Meaning, structure and visual activities
disappear, disappointed, elbowed, excited, frowned, polite, presented, problem, reason, stare, temper, unfriendly	about, after, doesn't, friend, knew, know, something, things, used, would	Phonemes /ai/ and /ə/ and /ow/	CD: Meaning, structure and visual activities
contents, cord, drill, finished, ingredients, inventions, inventors, junk, kennel, materials, problem, sketched, wound	asked, down, floor, good, idea, many, more, paper, thought, time, turns, work	Phoneme /ee/	CD: Meaning, structure and visual activities

Fast Lane band	Level	Book and author	Text type	Curriculum links	Word count
Purple	19	GIANT'S CAUSEWAY Julie Ellis	Retelling of a traditional folk story	Citizenship	642
Purple	19	VENUS BAY Julie Mitchell	Story with a familiar setting	Citizenship	587
Purple	19	BUZZ SEES THE DIFFERENCE Carmel Reilly	Story set in an imaginary world	Citizenship	696
Purple	19	TRAPPED Chris Bell	Story with a familiar setting	Citizenship	729
Purple	20	MAKING HEADLINES Carmel Reilly	Story in a familiar setting	Citizenship	758
Purple	20	DIRT ON MY SHOE Mike Graf	Adventure story	Science and Geography	693
Purple	20	GADGET BOY AND KID FANTASTIC George Ivanoff	Story set in an imaginary world	Citizenship	700
Purple	20	THE COAT Sharon Holt	Story with issues	Citizenship	726

Words in context	Frequently used words	Phonic opportunities	Related activity and assessment sheets
battles, causeway, contentedly, feeble, giant, giantess, Irish, might, nervous, pillowcase, pretend, ripping, Scotland, slabs, storming	because, behind, fighting, heavy, home, land, liked, live, near, path, strong, swim, water	Phoneme /f/	CD: Meaning, structure and visual activities
ambulance, cramped, currents, paddled, powerful, roared, searching, struck, surface, surfing, tumbling	before, board, brother, catch, down, easy, light, other, pulled, stand, thinking, through, wasn't, water, wrong	Phoneme /ee/	CD: Meaning, structure and visual activities
bomb, conference, creature, crowds, hideous, horrible, panic, peace, planet, president, represent, representative, spaceship, stampede, tripped, tumbled, whispered	because, everyone, finally, food, great, inside, laugh, something, strange, wasn't, when	Phoneme /ee/	CD: Meaning, structure and visual activities
bolted, clambered, cubicle, deserted, echoed, flicked, gulped, signal, snatched, stranded, stretched, survival, trapped, tugged, worried	about, again, asked, floor, help, laughed, learn, open, outside, school, sound, teacher, thought, walk	Phonemes /ch/ and /k/	CD: Meaning, structure and visual activities
biscuit, camera, classroom, collection, competition, computers, cuckoo, detention, editor, framed, groaned, guilty, headlines, newspaper, notebook, office, officers, photos, police, reporter, shots	although, exciting, listened, sneaking, strange, thought, towards, whatever, whispered, wonder, wrapped	Syllables	CD: Meaning, structure and visual activities
ancient, boulders, canyon, colourful, dinosaurs, families, fossilised, guided, jutted, microscope, paleontological, rainbow, ranger, ravine, sandstone, trail	added, alongside, answered, continued, explained, handful, minutes, responded, searched, sift, signs, suggested, those, tossing	Syllables	CD: Meaning, structure and visual activities
auditorium, badge, conference, crime-fighting, device, disappeared, disappearing, doctor, escape, hard-drive, international, sidekick, spotlight, spring-loaded, superhero, superheroes, superpower	compare, continued, faster, lady, reason, replied, similar, smiled, special, woman, worried, understand	Syllables	CD: Meaning, structure and visual activities
coat, conversation, decision, diamonds, dump, emeralds, garbage, locket, lurched, neighbour, pedal, photo, pockets, rubies, sobbing, trash, treasure, voices	angrily, daughter, emptied, faded, grey, louder, mistake, realised, repeat, spread, thought, thrown, ties, woman, years	Syllables	CD: Meaning, structure and visual activities

Fast Lane band	Level	Book and author	Text type	Curriculum links	Word count
Gold	21	BEARS IN CAMP Mike Graf	Graphic novel (adventure story)	Geography and Science	742
	21	NEW NEIGHBOURS Carmel Reilly	Mystery story	Design and Technology	793
	21	MY BEST FRIEND'S A GENIUS George Ivanoff	Story in a familiar setting	Design and Technology	853
	21	THE RIDDLE OF THE CAMEL RACE Nicolas Brasch	Story from another culture	Geography	711
	22	I WISH Jack Gabolinscy	Fantasy story	Citizenship	790
	22	MUDSLIDE Mike Graf	Graphic novel (adventure story)	Citizenship and Geography	881
	22	NICO'S LIST Julia Wall	Story with a familiar setting	Citizenship	834
	22	THE KEY CUTTER'S GRANDSON	Story dealing with issues	Citizenship	860

Words in context	Frequently used words	Phonic opportunities	Related activity and assessment sheets
airways, attacks, awake, bears, binoculars, campsite, commotion, grizzly, high-pitched, hike, iceberg, inhaler, lake, lungs, mountains, noise, pounds, relaxes, snowfield, trudge, valley, wheeze, whistling	across, adult, answer, arrive, blue, continues, distance, heading, its, passed, points, quickly, supposed, worry, young	Graphemes ng and ear	CD: Meaning, structure and visual activities
annoyed, blankets, crashing, curious, curtains, drifted, furniture, hammer, imagination, mysteries, neighbours, outlined, packages, peer, perfectly, promised, puppeteers, shadow, shuddered	again, appeared, brought, demanded, despite, disappoint, living, notice, ordinary, pieces, point, shrieked, strange, thought, through	Phonemes /ee/ and /oo/	CD: Meaning, structure and visual activities
aliens, Antarctica, article, automatic, brainy, crackle, electricity, feature, friend's, future, grounded, hyper-phone, logical, mobile, mouse-traps, oceanic, republic, sci-fi, unidentified, weird	answered, buy, dead, disappointed, explained, parents, point, shoulders, shrugging, strange, trouble, unless, you're	Phonemes /or/ and /k/	CD: Meaning, structure and visual activities
anxious, approached, camel, castle, challenge, cruel, duo, exist, failure, gestured, guarding, kingdom, lest, loser, prison, route, silver, subjects, sultan, sword, tattoo, tension, toenails	although, birthday, course, enough, exactly, leapt, meant, neither, once, ordered, roared, thought, trouble	Phonemes /oa/ and /j/	CD: Meaning, structure and visual activities
bobbing, bored, borrow, complained, cork, drawn, genie, high-five, impatient, moaned, rocked, rolled, sniffed, steered, stretched, subjects, yacht, yeah	across, another, bottle, friends, happy, months, other, quickly, school, somewhere, work	word ending: -ing	CD: Meaning, structure and visual activities
blaring, cliff, crumble, current, debris, La Nina, evacuated, footbridge, fumbled, loudspeaker, pavement, pelted, rescuers, sloshed, sprinted, super-sized, thrust, volume	afternoon, anything, behind, care, month, myself, once, river, suddenly, table	Phonemes /ee/ and /oo/	CD: Meaning, structure and visual activities
announcer, awesome, beloved, cancelled, courier, curious, entered, exactly, gross, jokingly, mooning, pretended, scowled, stomped	already, Friday, front, great, idea, know, last, sister, thought, through, turned, watched	Phonemes /s/ and /u/	CD: Meaning, structure and visual activities
bamboo, choices, crumpled, customer, excitement, huddled, muttered, pretended, properly, refused, scrunched, snatched, strain, swerved, tripping, yuan	above, around, began, bicycle, money, nothing, paper, path, slowly, square, through	Phoneme /oo/	CD: Meaning, structure and visual activities

Fast Lane band	Level	Book and author	Text type	Curriculum links	Word count
Silver	23	BRUNO'S TEA Julia Wall	Story with issues	Geography	1002
	23	IT'S A JUNGLE OUT THERE Peter Millett	Fantasy story	Science	959
	23	LIZZIE'S HIDDEN MESSAGE Julie Ellis	Story with issues	History	1045
	23	THE CONTEST Carmel Reilly	Graphic novel (myth)	History	878
	24	SHIPWRECK Carmel Reilly	Graphic novel (adventure story)	n/a	981
	24	DANNY'S DREAM Jack Gabolinscy	Story in a familiar setting	Physical Education	1014
	24	GOAL Peter Millett	Story with a familiar setting	Physical Education and Citizenship	1014
	24	MY BEST FRIEND THINKS I'M A GENIUS George Ivanoff	Fantasy story	Design and Technology	975

Words in context	Frequently used words	Phonic opportunities	Related activity and assessment sheets
affection, business, customer, deliveries, explained, furious, grateful, honour, imported, included, invited, liquid, mechanic, mystery, noticed, popular, radiators, regulars, reward, searching, tripped, university, whimper	already, although, around, bicycle, brought, each, knew, parents, people, school	Phonemes /ee/ and /oa/	CD: Meaning, structure and visual activities
awesome, bulged, commotion, complained, deluxe, famous, fantastic, hammock, magnificent, patio, petunias, queue, queuing, record, roaring, sprinted, stormed, success, tour, unbelievable	before, every, grass, money, outside, photos, suddenly, walk, world	Phonemes /ur/ and /or/	CD: Meaning, structure and visual activities
ancestor, attic, cabin, captured, chest, civil, curious, disappointed, essay, ordered, punished, quilt, seamstress, slave, slavery, tracking, treasure, valuable	because, enough, family, farmer, free, garden, nights, slave, thought, years	Grapheme th and phoneme /ai/	CD: Meaning, structure and visual activities
boast, challenge, clashed, creature, delicate, destroyed, determined, goddess, honour, insulted, jealous, original, powerful, prey, spinner, stubborn, tapestries, weaver, whipped	beautiful, better, goddess, lovely, teach, think, truth, wonderful, workshop, young	Phonemes /oo/ and /k/	CD: Meaning, structure and visual activities
abandon, branch, clearing, coconut, crackers, deck, dream, driftwood, imagining, jungle, life raft, loomed, lose, monkeys, packet, sail, scout, shipwreck, sign, stealing, stream, style, supplies, survived, swell, thirsty, weak, wildly, yacht	beautiful, believe, below, caught, closer, dried, enough, followed, goodness, guess, least, probably, sixth, someone's, sorry, watched	Graphemes wh and le	CD: Meaning, structure and visual activities
champion, cheering, cross country, dream, elbows, jogged, knobbly, lunchbox, marathon, medals, muscles, Olympic, popular, pranks, skinny, sprint, stadium, stride, style, television, victory	advised, altogether, blew, broke, crammed, dripping, enough, fifteen, further, joked, lengthened, matter, nervously, nine, proudly, raised, Saturday, second	Phoneme /ch/ and grapheme ou	CD: Meaning, structure and visual activities
deaf, defenders, dodged, dribbled, football, fouled, frustration, glare, glued, goalkeeper, launched, midfield, net, offside, onside, pitch, possession, precision, punched, referee, rocket, sideline, signal, skilfully, spotted, sprinted, swamped, tackled, team-mates, touchline, winger, wrist	able, anxiously, avoid, beaming, bellowed, blew, comfortable, communicate, delight, groaned, halfway, immediately, listen, lift, one, puffed, second, threw, through, unmarked, wide, won	Phoneme /or/ and grapheme g	CD: Meaning, structure and visual activities
actors, bald, blaze, clearing, costumes, device, electronics, engulfed, eyebrows, guy, headset, idea, jungle, matter, planning, platform, razor, screeching, squinted, teeth, tested, travelling, Tyrannosaurus rex, wires, zappy	accidentally, agreed, all right, become, belonged, blew, chanted, disappear, enter, greatest, hopefully, impossible, instant, reappear, somewhere, suggest, surrounded, towards, wide	Phonemes /e/ and /igh/	CD: Meaning, structure and visual activities

Fast Lane band	Level	Book and author	Text type	Curriculum links	Word count
Emerald	25	MORE LIKE HOME Carmel Reilly	Graphic novel (story with issues)	Citizenship and Geography	1054
	25	FIRE READY Michelle Vasiliu	Adventure story	Citizenship and Geography	1051
	25	MOON BUBBLE George Ivanoff	Fantasy story	Science and History	960
	25	NOT AGAIN Jack Gabolinscy	Story with issues	Citizenship	1033

Words in context	Frequently used words	Phonic opportunities	Related activity and assessment sheets
African, border, countryside, desperate, destroyed, exhausted, fear, gunshots, homeland, hope, journey, kidnapped, loss, migrate, numb, overcrowded, refugee, relative, sadness, screams, settle, shacks, soldiers, village, weather	allowed, aunt, choice, colour, completely, darkness, decide, farther, fought, language, months, ourselves, quickly, those, uncle, yourselves	Syllables	CD: Meaning, structure and visual activities
accident, agreed, ashen, calm, charred, cottage, crackled, darling, embers, forest, gutter, ladder, mesh, plugs, quote, season, shift, silence, smelt, smouldering, sunburnt, survival, sweeping, towels, towering, warn, weather, wilted, woollen	afterwards, approaching, describing, determined, exactly, extra, half, hour, necessary, possible, practised, quickly, strangely, wondered	Syllables	CD: Meaning, structure and visual activities
adventure, bubble, campfire, counts, crackled, craters, detector, egg, flame, flickered, floating, glowing, lifetime, loop, matches, mysterious, over-active, river, shimmering, silly, smooth, story, surface, treasure, zoomed	bright, decided, desperately, exactly, further, heading, hoping, problem, pulling, remembered, touched	Syllables	CD: Meaning, structure and visual activities
accident, accurate, ambulance, brain, coma, court, cowboys, damaged, determined, expensive, fortune, hospital, microwave, screech, shoulders, showered, stammered, toast, unconscious, weights, wheelchair, wrestle	hour, hurry, importantly, laughed, lying, middle, month, parents, perfect, position, practice, quickly, racing, slow, strange, strengthen	Syllables	CD: Meaning, structure and visual activities

Reading Record

Ben Fox Saves the Day   Level 6 Yellow

Name: _____ Date: _____ Age: _____

Text: _Ben Fox Saves the Day_   Level: ___6___

R.W.: ___104___   Accuracy: _____   S.C. Rate: _____

Page			E	S.C.	Errors MSV	Self-corrections MSV
4	One day, Ben Fox went to the shop for his mum.	11				
	He was outside the shop	16				
	getting oranges out of a box,	22				
	when the woman from the shop shouted,	29				
	"Stop him! Stop him!"	33				
	Ben looked up at the woman.	39				
5	"See that boy running away!"	44				
	she shouted. "He has my bag!"	50				
	Ben looked down the street.	55				
6	"I can see a boy.	60				
	He has a blue top and black shorts on	69				
	and he has a red bag," Ben said.	77				
	"Yes, that is him," said the woman.	84				
7	"And that is my bag!"	89				
	"Stay here," said Ben to the woman.	96				
	"I will get your bag back for you."	104				
Total:						

Reading Record Assessment

Ben Fox Saves the Day   Level 6 Yellow

Name: _____

Reading Level: _____

Accuracy level: _____ = 1: _____ = _____%

Self-correction rate: _____ = _____ = 1: _____   Easy/Instructional/Hard

Questions to Check for Understanding

Literal

1. What does the woman shout when the boy takes her bag?   Yes/No
   (The woman shouts "Stop him! Stop him!")
2. What colour are the boy's shorts?   Yes/No
   (The boy's shorts are black.)

Inferential

1. Why does Ben chase the boy?   Yes/No
   (Ben chases the boy because he has stolen the woman's bag.)
2. What else could Ben have bought from the fruit shop?   Yes/No
   (Ben could also have bought watermelon, pears, lettuce, tomatoes and bananas from the fruit shop.)

Response

1. How would you feel if someone stole your bag?   Valid/Invalid
   (Response answers will vary.)

Analysis of reading behaviours (meaning, structural and visual information, self-monitoring, self-correcting, fluency)

_____
_____
_____
_____
_____

Phonics Assessment

Level 6 Yellow

Name: _____

Age: _____ **Date:** _____

man	flan	
top	stop	shop
day	stay	
boy	ploy	
far	star	chart
her	stern	
tow	blow	show
out	cloud	shout
seat	treat	wheat
year	clear	shear
hair	stair	chair
bake	flake	shake
sing	sting	thing

Frequently Used Words Assessment

Level 6 Yellow

Name: _____

Age: _____   **Date:** _____

after	again	around	away
came	children	come	down
eat	first	friend	gave
have	here	house	how
inside	little	look	made
make	more	new	night
out	over	people	said
school	some	stay	take
these	they	time	under
very	want	was	what
when	where	who	you
your	can't	don't	I'm
it's	I've		

Comprehension Assessment Fiction

Level 6 Yellow

Name: _____ Age: _____ Date: _____

Ben Fox Saves the Day ✓ or ✗

1. What does the woman shout when the boy takes her bag? (literal)
   _____ ☐
   _____

2. What colour are the boy's shorts? (literal)
   _____ ☐
   _____

3. What are the children playing on in the park? (literal)
   _____ ☐
   _____

4. Why does Ben chase the boy? (inferential)
   _____ ☐
   _____

5. What else could Ben have bought at the fruit shop? (inferential)
   _____ ☐
   _____

6. In what places does the story take place? (inferential)
   _____ ☐
   _____

7. Do you think the way Ben stops the thief is clever? Why? (response)
   _____ Valid/
   _____ Invalid

8. How would you feel if someone stole your bag? (response)
   _____ Valid/
   _____ Invalid

9. Why do you think the boy steals the bag? (response)
   _____ Valid/
   _____ Invalid

Yellow Band Placement Sheet

Level 6 Yellow

Name: _____ Age: _____ Date: _____

Fluency and Accuracy		Correct words per minute	Accuracy Rate	Self-correction Rate
	Text 1		%	1:
	Text 2		%	1:
Comments on the information systems	Meaning Structure Visual			
Reading Record Comprehension	Literal 1. 2.			✓/✗ ✓/✗
	Inferential 1. 2.			✓/✗ ✓/✗
	Response 1.			Valid/Invalid
Phonics Assessment	Combinations to be learned an, op, ay, oy, ar, er, ow, ou, eat, ear, air, ake, ing			___ /13
	Blends to be learned fl, st, pl, bl, cl, tr			___ /13
	Digraphs to be learned sh, ch, wh, th			___ /9
Frequently Used Words Assessment	after, came, eat, have, inside, make, out, school, these, very, when, your, it's, again, children, first, here, little, more, over, some, they, want, where, can't, I've, around, come, friend, house, look, new, people, stay, time, was, who, don't, away, down, gave, how, made, night, said, take, under, what, you, I'm			___ /50
Comprehension Assessment	1. 2. 3. 4. 5. 6. 7. 8. 9.			✓/✗ ✓/✗ ✓/✗ ✓/✗ ✓/✗ ✓/✗ Valid/Invalid Valid/Invalid Valid/Invalid

Reading Record

Magic Tricks   Level 9 Blue

Name: _____   Date: _____   Age: _____

Text: *Magic Tricks* _____   Level: ___9___

R.W.: ___138_____   Accuracy: _____   S.C. Rate: _____

Page			E	S.C.	Errors MSV	Self-corrections MSV
8	At last, it was Mick's turn.	6				
	He set up a little table	12				
	in the middle of the stage.	18				
	He put two hats and some rings	25				
	on the table.	28				
9	He could see his family in front of him.	37				
	He could see all his friends.	43				
	Everyone was quiet.	46				
	They were waiting for him to start.	53				
10	Mick opened out his cape.	58				
	"TA-DA!" he called.	61				
	He was going to pull out some flowers,	69				
	but his cape got stuck	74				
	on the side of the table.	80				
11	The table crashed down.	84				
	The hats and rings fell on the floor.	92				
	Everyone laughed as Mick raced	97				
	to pick everything up.	101				
12	Mick put everything back and started again.	108				
	This time, he was going to do	115				
	the joining-the-rings trick.	120				
	He put them one way.	125				
	Then he put them another way.	131				
	But the rings would not join up.	138				
Total						

Reading Record Assessment

Magic Tricks   Level 9 Blue

Name: _____

Reading Level: _____

Accuracy level: _____ = 1: _____ = _____ %

Self-correction rate: _____ = _____ = 1: _____   Easy/Instructional/Hard

Questions to Check for Understanding

Literal

1. How many hats does Mick put on the table?   Yes/No
   (Mick puts two hats on the table.)
2. Who can Mick see in front of him?   Yes/No
   (Mick can see his mum and dad and all his friends in front of him.)

Inferential

1. How many rings does Mick have?   Yes/No
   (Mick has three rings.)
2. Why does everyone laugh at Mick?   Yes/No
   (Everyone laughs at Mick because he gets his cape stuck and his tricks go wrong.)

Response

1. Do you think Mick is nervous about performing on stage?
   Why or why not?   Valid/Invalid
   (Answers will vary)

Analysis of reading behaviours (meaning cues, structural cues, visual information, self-monitoring, self-correcting, fluency)

_____
_____
_____
_____
_____

Phonics Assessment

Level 9 Blue

Name: _____

Age: _____ **Date:** _____

goat	float	
dark	stark	shark
cool	spoon	shoot
now	clown	
day	stay	
back	stack	whack
pain	claim	chain
lick	brick	thick
sing	sting	thing
tame	blame	shame
hop	drop	chop
land	plan	than
long	prong	thong
night	fright	

Frequently Used Words Assessment

Level 9 Blue

Name: _____

Age: _____   Date: _____

her	fast	look	next
out	she	so	stop
said	went	with	away
but	could	called	day
going	he	his	last
on	of	put	was
did	good	like	me
really	then	had	you
around	made	get	no
not	want	were	then
that	make	they	have
are	me	people	push
for	and		

Comprehension Assessment Fiction

Level 9 Blue

Name: _____ Age: _____ Date: _____

Magic Tricks ✓ or ✗

1. What does Mick make to wear at the school concert? (literal)

2. What happens to the dancing girls? (literal)

3. What does Mick pull out of his hat? (literal)

4. Do you think Mick is scared on stage? How can you tell? (inferential)

5. Why are the crowd laughing and clapping? (inferential)

6. Why does Mick think he is a bad magician? (inferential)

7. How do you think Mick feels when none of his tricks work? (response)

   Valid/Invalid

8. Do you think Mick will put his hand up to do something at the next school concert? Why or why not? (response)

   Valid/Invalid

9. Would it be more difficult to perform in front of a mirror or in front of other people? Why? (response)

   Valid/Invalid

Blue Band Placement Sheet
Level 9 Blue

Name: _____ Age: _____ Date: _____

Fluency and Accuracy		Correct words per minute	Accuracy Rate	Self-correction Rate
	Text 1		%	1:
	Text 2		%	1:
Comments on the information systems	Meaning Structure Visual			
Reading Record Comprehension	Literal 1. 2.			✓/✗ ✓/✗
	Inferential 1. 2.			✓/✗ ✓/✗
	Response 1.			Valid/Invalid
Phonics Assessment	Combinations to be learned oa, ar, oo, ow, ay, ack, ai, ick, ing, ame, op, an, ong, igh			___/14
	Blends to be learned fl, st, sp, cl, br, bl, dr, pl, pr, fr			___/14
	Digraphs to be learned sh, wh, ch, th			___/10
Frequently Used Words Assessment	her, out, said, but, going, on, did, really, around, not, that, are, for, fast, she, went, could, he, of, good, then, made, want, make, me, and, look, so, with, called, his, put, like, had, get, were, they, people, next, stop, away, day, last, was, me, you, no, then, have, push			___/50
Comprehension Assessment	1. 2. 3. 4. 5. 6. 7. 8. 9.			✓/✗ ✓/✗ ✓/✗ ✓/✗ ✓/✗ ✓/✗ Valid/Invalid Valid/Invalid Valid/Invalid

Reading Record

The Game   Level 12 Green

Name: _____   Date: _____   Age: _____

Text: _The Game_____   Level: ___12___

R.W.: ____157_____   Accuracy: _____   S.C. Rate: _____

Page			E	S.C.	Errors MSV	Self-corrections MSV
16	Michael looked out of the cave.	6				
	"Run!" he shouted.	9				
	The two boys ran quickly.	14				
	"There's the control tower!"	18				
	shouted Michael.	20				
	"Let's go!" shouted Brad.	24				
17	Suddenly, a giant cyborg stepped out	30				
	from behind a tree.	34				
19	Brad rolled over on the ground and ran	42				
	at the cyborg. He jumped onto its back.	50				
	The cyborg swooped and grabbed at Brad.	57				
	It tried to shake him off.	63				
	Brad pulled out a pen and jammed it	71				
	into the cyborg's control panel.	76				
	The cyborg started to shake and spin.	83				
	Then, it fell to the ground.	89				
20	"Run to the control tower!" shouted Brad.	96				
21	Brad and Michael ran to the control tower.	104				
	Brad put the disk in.	109				
	He started to shut down the game.	116				
	A red light started flashing.	121				
22	But, suddenly, another cyborg	125				
	came out from behind a rock.	131				
	"Take my hand!" shouted Brad.	136				
23	Brad pushed the flashing red light.	142				
	Suddenly, there was a loud noise.	148				
	Brad and Michael spun around.	153				
	They turned upside down.	157				
Total:						

Reading Record Assessment

The Game   Level 12 Green

Name: _____

Reading Level: _____

Accuracy level: _____ = 1: _____ = _____%

Self-correction rate: _____ = _____ = 1: _____   Easy/Instructional/Hard

Questions to Check for Understanding

Literal

1. What jumps out from behind a tree?   Yes/No
   (A cyborg jumps out from behind the tree.)
2. What happens when Brad jams a pen in the cyborg's control panel?   Yes/No
   (When Brad jams a pen in the cyborg's control panel, it starts to shake and spin, then it falls to the ground.)

Inferential

1. How does Michael know where the control tower is?   Yes/No
   (Michael knows where the control tower is because he can see it in the distance.)
2. How does Brad know where the cyborg's control panel is?   Yes/No
   (Brad knows where the cyborg's control because he has played the game before.)

Response

1. What would you do if you were faced by a cyborg?   Valid/Invalid
   (Answers will vary.)

Analysis of reading behaviours (meaning, structural and visual information, self-monitoring, self-correcting, fluency)

_____
_____
_____
_____
_____

Phonics Assessment

Level 12 Green

Name: _____

Age: _____   Date: _____

cow	crowd	
born	store	thorn
way	play	
team	speak	cheat
hail	trail	
coin	spoil	
round	cloud	shout
need	tree	sheep
long	wrong	thong
rock	stock	shock
sing	bring	thing
call	small	
year	clear	shear
her	stern	

Frequently Used Words Assessment

Level 12 Green

Name: _____

Age: _____ Date: _____

each	always	guess	suddenly
along	soon	right	quickly
being	only	move	through
very	people	feed	few
more	around	better	past
many	almost	forever	would
same	table	sort	alone
began	stay	also	walk
because	need	that	gave
join	grow	most	wants
fall	alive	are	know
again	made	were	knew
saves	where		

Comprehension Assessment Fiction

Level 12 Green

Name: _____ Age: _____ Date: _____

The Game
✓ or ✗

1. What does Brad hear through his headphones? (literal)
   _____ ☐
   _____

2. Why do Brad and Michael run into a cave? (literal)
   _____ ☐
   _____

3. How do the boys know where the control tower is? (literal)
   _____ ☐
   _____

4. How do you think Michael feels about being inside the game? (inferential)
   _____ ☐
   _____

5. Who or what do you think is firing the red laser? (inferential)
   _____ ☐
   _____

6. How do you think Michael feels at the end of the story? (inferential)
   _____ ☐
   _____

7. Do you think Brad is brave? Why or why not? (response)
   _____
   _____ Valid/Invalid

8. Do you like this game? Would you like to play it? Give reasons for your answer. (response)
   _____
   _____ Valid/Invalid

9. What game would you like to be inside? (response)
   _____
   _____ Valid/Invalid

Green Band Placement Sheet

Level 12 Green

Name: _____ Age: _____ Date: _____

Fluency and Accuracy		Correct words per minute	Accuracy Rate	Self-correction Rate
	Text 1		%	1:
	Text 2		%	1:
Comments on the information systems	Meaning			
	Structure			
	Visual			
Reading Record Comprehension	Literal 1. 2.			✓/✗ ✓/✗
	Inferential 1. 2.			✓/✗ ✓/✗
	Response 1.			Valid/Invalid
Phonics Assessment	Combinations to be learned ow, or, ay, ea, ai, oi, ou, ee, ong, ck, ing, all, ear, er			___/14
	Blends to be learned cr, st, pl, sp, tr, cl, wr, br, sm			___/14
	Digraphs to be learned th, ch, sh, wh			___/8
Frequently Used Words Assessment	each, along, being, very, more, many, same, began, because, join, fall, again, saves, always, soon, only, people, around, almost, table, stay, need, grow, alive, made, where, guess, right, move, feed, better, forever, sort, also, that, most, are, were, suddenly, quickly, through, few, past, would, alone, walk, gave, wants, know, knew,			___/50
Comprehension Assessment	1. 2. 3. 4. 5. 6. 7. 8. 9.			✓/✗ ✓/✗ ✓/✗ ✓/✗ ✓/✗ ✓/✗ Valid/Invalid Valid/Invalid Valid/Invalid

Reading Record

The Golden Touch   Level 15 Orange

Name: _____   Date: _____   Age: _____

Text: _The Golden Touch_   Level: ___15___

R.W.: ___145___   Accuracy: _____   S.C. Rate: _____

Page			E	S.C.	Errors MSV	Self-corrections MSV
8	King Midas took pity on the man	7				
	and took him back to the palace.	14				
	There, he made sure that the man had	22				
	lots of food and drink. He also gave him	31				
	a warm bed to sleep in, for ten days.	40				
9	At the end of the ten days,	47				
	King Midas gave the man some money	54				
	and sent him on his way.	60				
	The man was very grateful.	65				
10	Watching over this act of kindness	71				
	was Dionysus, one of the Gods.	77				
	Dionysus appeared before King Midas	82				
	and said, "Your act of kindness	88				
	will be rewarded. I grant you one wish."	96				
12	King Midas saw that, finally,	101				
	he had a chance to be richer than	109				
	all the other kings he knew.	115				
	"I want everything I touch	120				
	to turn to gold," he told Dionysus.	127				
13	"I'm not sure that's such a good idea,"	135				
	Dionysus said. "Are you sure	140				
	you don't want something else?"	145				
Total:						

Reading Record Assessment

The Golden Touch   Level 15 Orange

Name: _____

Reading Level: _____

Accuracy level: _____ = 1: _____ = _____%

Self-correction rate: _____ = _____ = 1: _____   Easy/Instructional/Hard

Questions to Check for Understanding

Literal

1. How does King Midas treat the man he finds in the palace garden?   Yes/No
(King Midas makes sure the man has lots of food and drink and a warm bed to sleep in.)

2. How is King Midas's act of kindness rewarded?   Yes/No
(King Midas's kindness is rewarded by Dionysus granting him a wish.)

Inferential

1. Why does King Midas give the man some money?   Yes/No
(King Midas gives the man some money so he can live.)

2. How does the man show his gratitude to King Midas?   Yes/No
(The man shows his gratitude to Kind Midas by bowing and shaking his hand.)

Response

1. Do you think King Midas deserves to be rewarded for his act of kindness? Why or why not?   Valid/Invalid
(Answers will vary.)

Analysis of reading behaviours (meaning, structural and visual information, self-monitoring, self-correcting, fluency)

_____
_____
_____
_____
_____
_____

Phonics Assessment

Level 15 Orange

Name: _____

Age: _____   Date: _____

wanted	started	chewed
lunches	dresses	
environmental	global	
warming	blowing	shouting
government		
babies	stories	cherries
leaves	sleeves	themselves
nearly	slowly	quickly
letter	clever	shopper
helpful	grateful	
kindness	blindness	
highest	slowest	cheapest

Frequently Used Words Assessment

Level 15 Orange

Name: _____

Age: _____ Date: _____

always	seen	look	each
move	knows	good	already
kinds	many	also	knew
about	sometimes	gives	next
across	because	around	house
their	our	little	keep
they	last	even	gave
come	much	first	hours
other	might	name	everything
three	more	part	over
new	could	again	too
years	hard	asked	such
been	known		

Comprehension Assessment Fiction

Level 15 Orange

Name: _____ Age: _____ Date: _____

The Golden Touch ✓ or ✗

1. What is the one downfall of King Midas? (literal) _____

2. What is King Midas's wish? (literal) _____

3. What happens when King Midas asks his daughter to feed him? (literal) _____

4. Why do you think the man King Midas finds in the palace garden thinks he is in big trouble when he meets the king? (inferential) _____

5. Why do you think Dionysus doesn't think King Midas's wish is such a good idea? (inferential) _____

6. What things do you think King Midas would consider more important than money at the end of the story? (inferential) _____

7. Imagine you are King Midas and Dionysus is offering you one wish. What would your one wish be? Explain your choice. (response) _____
   Valid/Invalid

8. Do you think people should always be rewarded for doing an act of kindness? Give reasons for your answer. (response) _____
   Valid/Invalid

9. Make a list of all the things you consider to be more important than money on the back of this page. Provide one reason for each item you list. (response)
   Valid/Invalid

Orange Band Placement Sheet

Level 15 Orange

Name: _____ **Age:** _____ **Date:** _____

Fluency and Accuracy		Correct words per minute	Accuracy Rate	Self-correction Rate
	Text 1		%	1:
	Text 2		%	1:
Comments on the information systems	Meaning Structure Visual			
Reading Record Comprehension	Literal 1. 2.			✓/✗ ✓/✗
	Inferential 1. 2.			✓/✗ ✓/✗
	Response 1.			Valid/Invalid
Phonics Assessment	Combinations to be learned ed, es, al, ing, ment, ies, ves, ly, er, ful, ness, est			___/12
	Blends to be learned st, dr, gl, bl, sl, cl, gr			___/11
	Digraphs to be learned ch, sh, th, qu			___/7
Frequently Used Words Assessment	always, move, kinds, about, across, their, they, come, other, three, new, years, been, seen, knows, many, sometimes, because, our, last, much, might, more, could, hard, known, look, good, also, gives, around, little, even, first, name, part, again, asked, each, already, knew, next, house, keep, gave, hours, everything, over, too, such			___/50
Comprehension Assessment	1. 2. 3. 4. 5. 6. 7. 8. 9.			✓/✗ ✓/✗ ✓/✗ ✓/✗ ✓/✗ ✓/✗ Valid/Invalid Valid/Invalid Valid/Invalid

Reading Record

Inside the Gate   Level 17 Turquoise

Name: _____ Date: _____ Age: _____

Text: _Inside the Gate_____   Level: ___17___

R.W.: ____148_____   Accuracy: _____   S.C. Rate: _____

Page			E	S.C.	Errors MSV	Self-corrections MSV
4	Today it is dusty outside.	5				
	The wind is whipping at the earth	12				
	and sending clouds of brown dirt	18				
	all around the town.	22				
	I sit here on the doorstep	28				
	and watch the women come back from work.	36				
	Finally, I see Grandma carrying	41				
	her basket.	43				
	She is covered in dust and looks tired,	51				
	but she smiles when she sees me.	58				
	"What are you up to, Kemzie?"	64				
	she asks.	66				
5	"Waiting for you!" I say.	71				
	"I want you to come	76				
	and help me plant trees."	81				
	"Trees?" asks Grandma.	84				
6	I tell Grandma that someone came	90				
	to speak to us at school today	97				
	about tree planting.	100				
	I tell her I want to help out	108				
	in the nursery just out of town	115				
	where they grow the trees.	120				
	"We need the trees to give us wood,	128				
	shade and fruit,	131				
	and to help keep the Earth well,"	138				
	I say quickly.	141				
7	Grandma laughs,	143				
	and puts her basket down.	148				
Total:						

Reading Record Assessment

Inside the Gate   Level 17 Turquoise

Name: _____

Reading level: _____

Accuracy level: _____ = 1: _____ = _____%

Self-correction rate: _____ = _____ = 1: _____   Easy/Instructional/Hard

Questions to Check for Understanding

Literal
1. Where is Kemzie sitting?   Yes/No
   (Kemzie is sitting on the doorstep.)
2. Why can't Grandma go with Kemzie to help out in the nursery?   Yes/No
   (Grandma can't go with Kemzie to help out in the nursery because
   she has to make dinner.)

Inferential
1. How is Grandma carrying her basket?   Valid/Invalid
   (Grandma is carrying her basket on her head.)
2. Why is Grandma covered in dust?   Valid/Invalid
   (Grandma is covered in dust because it is dusty in the town today.)

Response
1. Why do you think Kemzie wants her grandma to go with her
   to the nursery?   Valid/Invalid

Analysis of reading behaviours (meaning, structural and visual information, self-monitoring, self-correcting, fluency)

_____
_____
_____
_____
_____
_____
_____

Phonics Assessment

Level 17 Turquoise

Name: _____

Age: _____ **Date:** _____

wood	stool	should
town	clouds	
heard	blur	whispered
cage		change
desk	tricks	quickly
head	steady	
home	grow	show
causes	transport	chore
carpet	grass	
cent	scientists	
people	steel	wheel

Frequently Used Words Assessment

Level 17 Turquoise

Name: _____

Age: _____ Date: _____

another	asks	because	become
behind	between	body	could
couldn't	covered	enough	group
huge	inside	new	know
large	living	loudly	mean
might	million	knew	other
own	provide	say	someone
speak	special	sure	their
there's	they're	third	three
tiny	too	tough	towards
upper	use	while	whispered
who	without	women	work
would	yourself		

Comprehension Assessment
Fiction

Level 17 Turquoise

Name: _____ Age: _____ Date: _____

Inside the Gate ✓ or ✗

1. What does Kemzie tell Grandma she wants to do? (inferential)
   _____
   _____ ☐

2. What are people doing at the back of the nursery? (literal)
   _____
   _____ ☐

3. What does Makena come round with? (literal)
   _____
   _____ ☐

4. Why is the nursery like "a sea of green"? (inferential)
   _____
   _____ ☐

5. Where does Kemzie meet the person who came to speak to her class at school about tree planting? (inferential)
   _____
   _____ ☐

6. Why does Kemzie like working at the nursery with her friend Anne? (inferential)
   _____
   _____ ☐

7. What sort of person do you think Makena is? (response)
   _____
   _____ Valid/Invalid

8. Imagine you are Grandma. Would you feel angry or proud when Kemzie goes to the nursery? Explain your choice. (response)
   _____
   _____ Valid/Invalid

9. What message about trees is conveyed in this story? (response)
   _____
   _____ Valid/Invalid

Turquoise Band Placement Sheet
Level 17 Turquoise

Name: _____ Age: _____ Date: _____

Fluency and Accuracy		Correct words per minute	Accuracy Rate	Self-correction Rate
	Text 1		%	1:
	Text 2		%	1:
Comments on the information systems	Meaning Structure Visual			
Reading Record Comprehension	Literal 1. 2.			Yes/No Yes/No
	Inferential 1. 2.			Yes/No Yes/No
	Response 1.			Valid/Invalid
Phonics Assessment	Combinations to be learned oo, ou, ow, er, soft g, hard c, ea, long o, or, ar, soft c, long e			___ /11
	Blends to be learned st, cl, bl, tr, gr, sc			___ /10
	Digraphs to be learned sh, wh, ch, qu			___ /7
Frequently Used Words Assessment	another, behind, couldn't, huge, large, might, own, speak, there's, tiny, upper, who, would, asks, between, covered, inside, living, million, provide, special, they're, too, use, without, yourself, because, body, enough, new, loudly, knew, say, sure, third, tough, while, women, become, could, group, know, mean, other, someone, their, three, towards, whispered, work			___ /50
Comprehension Assessment	1. 2. 3. 4. 5. 6. 7. 8. 9.			✓/✗ ✓/✗ ✓/✗ ✓/✗ ✓/✗ ✓/✗ Valid/Invalid Valid/Invalid Valid/Invalid

Reading Record

Buzz Sees the Difference   Level 19 Purple

Name: _____   Date: _____   Age: _____

Text: _Buzz Sees the Difference_   Level: __19__

R.W.: __153__   Accuracy: _____   S.C. Rate: _____

Page		E	S.C.	Errors MSV	Self-corrections MSV
8	Buzz and Zip followed the crowd across a square to 10				
	a huge hall. "I think I need something to eat," Buzz 21				
	said as they were about to go inside. 29				
	"Buzz, this is a peace conference," said Zip. 37				
	"You need to start thinking about what we've 45				
	all got in common." 49				
9	"Not much, by the look of them," said Buzz, who 59				
	was always in a bad mood when he was hungry. 69				
10	Buzz found a food stand run by the representatives 78				
	from planet Juno. The food looked very strange, 86				
	but tasted quite good. 90				
	Buzz took his food to the other side of the square, 101				
	and sat down next to a wall. He was happy to be 113				
	away from the crowds. 117				
11	Suddenly, he heard a voice coming from the other 126				
	side of the wall. "Have you seen how hideous most 136				
	of them are?" it whispered. "Just think how much 145				
	better they'll look when we blow them up!" 153				
Total:					

Reading Record Assessment

Buzz Sees the Difference   Level 19 Purple

Name: _____

Reading level: _____

Accuracy level: _____ = 1: _____ = _____%

Self-correction rate: _____ = _____ = 1: _____   Easy/Instructional/Hard

Questions to Check for Understanding

Literal
1. Where are Buzz and Zip?   Yes/No
   (Buzz and Zip are at a peace conference.)
2. What does Buzz overhear a voice say?   Yes/No
   (Buzz overhears a voice say that everyone at the peace conference is hideous but they will look better when they are blown up.)

Inferential
1. Why does Buzz think the food at the food stand is very strange?   Yes/No
   (Buzz thinks the food at the food stand is strange because he isn't used to it.)
2. What does the voice Buzz overhears mean when it says everyone is hideous?   Yes/No
   (The voice means that everyone is ugly.)

Response
1. Why do you think Zip tells Buzz to think about what he has in common with everyone?   Valid/Invalid

Analysis of reading behaviours (meaning, structural and visual information, self-monitoring, self-correcting, fluency)

_____
_____
_____
_____
_____
_____
_____
_____

Phonics Assessment

Level 19 Purple

Name: _____

Age: _____ Date: _____

fight	afraid
	off
photograph	telephone
chance	such
school	ached
	think
	kinds
protect	collection
earth	other
start	most

Frequently Used Words Assessment

Level 19 Purple

Name: _____

Age: _____   Date: _____

because	thought	together	makes
everyone	before	objects	much
finally	down	away	think
inside	things	every	under
wasn't	thinking	more	used
when	through	most	were
behind	water	where	enough
near	different	which	never
about	people	around	known
again	their	doing	also
asked	work	goes	something
open	years	live	great
outside	another		

Comprehension Assessment
Fiction

Level 19 Purple

Name: _____ Age: _____ Date: _____

Buzz Sees the Difference ✓ or ✗

1. What does the president of planet Zero tell Buzz and Zip to do? (literal)
   _____ ☐

2. How does Buzz let everyone know about the bomb? (literal) _____
   _____ ☐

3. Why doesn't the thin, strange creature hear Buzz? (literal) _____
   _____ ☐

4. Why does Zip cut Buzz off when they are speaking to the president of planet Zero? (inferential)
   _____
   _____ ☐

5. Why does Zip not believe Buzz when Buzz tells him about the bomb? (inferential)
   _____
   _____ ☐

6. What does Zip look like? (inferential)
   _____
   _____ ☐

7. Do you think Buzz doesn't want to attend the peace conference? (response)
   _____
   _____ Valid/Invalid

8. Imagine you are Zip. Would you believe Buzz when he told you there was a bomb in the room? Why or why not? (response)
   _____
   _____ Valid/Invalid

9. What is the message of this text about differences in people? (response)
   _____
   _____ Valid/Invalid

Purple Band Placement Sheet

Level 19 Purple

Name: _____ Age: _____ Date: _____

Fluency and Accuracy		Correct words per minute	Accuracy Rate	Self-correction Rate
	Text 1		%	1:
	Text 2		%	1:
Comments on the information systems	Meaning Structure Visual			
Reading Record Comprehension	Literal 1. 2.			Yes/No Yes/No
	Inferential 1. 2.			Yes/No Yes/No
	Response 1.			Valid/Invalid
Phonics Assessment	Combinations to be learned f, ff, ph, ch, ch = hard *c*, nk, nd, ct, er, st			___ /7
				___ /10
Frequently Used Words Assessment	because, everyone, finally, inside, wasn't, when, behind, near, about, again, asked, open, outside, thought, before, down, things, thinking, through, water, different, people, their, work, years, another, together, objects, away, every, more, most, where, which, around, doing, goes, live, makes, much, think, under, used, were, enough, never, known, also, something, great			___ /50
Comprehension Assessment	1. 2. 3. 4. 5. 6. 7. 8. 9.			✓/✗ ✓/✗ ✓/✗ ✓/✗ ✓/✗ ✓/✗ Valid/Invalid Valid/Invalid Valid/Invalid

Reading Record

The Riddle of the Camel Race   Level 21 Gold

Name: _____   Date: _____   Age: _____

Text: _The Riddle of the Camel Race_   Level: _21_

R.W.: _159_   Accuracy: _____   S.C. Rate: _____

Page		E	S.C.	Errors MSV	Self-corrections MSV
4	Once upon a time, in a land so far away that it could 13 only be reached by a supersonic jet (although, of course, 23 supersonic jets didn't exist back then), there lived a very 33 cruel sultan. This sultan ruled his kingdom with an iron 43 fist. It really was an iron fist, because he had lost one 55 hand in a sword fight and had ordered the best doctor 66 in the kingdom to fit him with an iron hand. 76				
6	Everyone in the land did exactly what the sultan 85 ordered. They were too afraid not to. The kingdom's 94 prisons were full of subjects who had not done exactly 104 what the sultan had ordered or had not done it 114 fast enough. 116				
8	For most of the year, the sultan ordered his people 126 to do normal kingdom-type jobs – guarding his castle, 134 hunting for his food, cleaning his silver and clipping 143 his toenails. 145				
9	But, once a year, on his birthday, the sultan had a 156 bit of fun. 159				
Total:					

Reading Record Assessment

The Riddle of the Camel Race   Level 21 Gold

Name: _____

Reading level: _____

Accuracy level: _____ = 1: _____ = _____%

Self-correction rate: _____ = _____ = 1: _____

Easy/Instructional/Hard

Questions to Check for Understanding

Literal
1. How did the sultan lose his hand?   Yes/No
   (The sultan lost his hand in a sword fight.)
2. What are four normal kingdom-type jobs the sultan orders his people to do?   Yes/No
   (Four normal kingdom-type jobs the sultan orders his people to do are: guarding his castle, hunting for his food, cleaning his silver and clipping his toenails.)

Inferential
1. How does the adjective 'iron-fisted' suit the sultan's personality?   Yes/No
   (The adjective 'iron-fisted' suits the sultan's personality because he is very cruel.)
2. How does the sultan make sure his subjects complete the challenge he sets each year?   Yes/No
   (The sultan makes sure his subjects complete his challenge each year by making it known that if a subject turns down a challenge, he or she will spend many years in prison.)

Response
1. Would you like to be one of this sultan's subjects? Why or why not?   Valid/Invalid

Analysis of reading behaviours (meaning, structural and visual information, self-monitoring, self-correcting, fluency)

_____
_____
_____
_____
_____
_____
_____

Phonics Assessment

Level 21 Gold

Name: _____

Age: _____   **Date:** _____

bear	flair	their
to	group	
talk	floor	thought
leapt	breakfast	check
farther	star	sharp
birthday	stir	whirl
human	clue	
century		
high	skies	pupil
rain	prey	
baby	stage	they

Frequently Used Words Assessment

Level 21 Gold

Name: _____

Age: _____   Date: _____

she's	through	throughout	similar
who's	demanded	century	third
you're	although	ideas	areas
unless	enough	prove	feed
across	exactly	included	female
answer	once	order	grows
its	history	otherwise	stays
answered	including	population	appears
that'll	often	unable	proven
rather	usually	colourful	studying
again	within	least	survive
shrieked	examples	million	threat
thought	area		

Comprehension Assessment
Fiction

Level 21 Gold

Name: _____ Age: _____ Date: _____

The Riddle of the Camel Race ✓ or ✗

1. Who fitted the sultan with his iron hand? (literal) ☐

2. What will happen to the loser of the challenge the sultan sets Ali and Omar? (literal) ☐

3. Who approaches Ali and Omar during the race? (literal) ☐

4. Why does everyone in the kingdom stay in bed on the morning of the sultan's birthday? (inferential) ☐

5. Why does the sultan have a huge grin on his face when he tells Ali and Omar about the challenge? (inferential) ☐

6. How does Shiraz's advice help Ali and Omar? (inferential) ☐

7. What do you think the sultan would say if he knew Shiraz had helped Ali and Omar? (response)

   Valid/Invalid

8. Why do you think Shiraz helps the men? (response)

   Valid/Invalid

9. What do you think of the way the sultan runs his kingdom? (response)

   Valid/Invalid

Gold Band Placement Sheet

Level 21 Gold

Name: _____ Age: _____ Date: _____

Fluency and Accuracy		Correct words per minute	Accuracy Rate	Self-correction Rate
	Text 1		%	1:
	Text 2		%	1:
Comments on the information systems	Meaning Structure Visual			
Reading Record Comprehension	Literal 1. 2.			Yes/No Yes/No
	Inferential 1. 2.			Yes/No Yes/No
	Response 1.			Valid/Invalid
Phonics Assessment	Phonic combinations to be learned air, long *o*, or, e, ar, er, long *u*, soft *c*, long *i*, ay, long *a*			___ /11
	Blends to be learned fl, gr, br, st, ci, sk, pr			___ /10
	Digraphs to be learned th, ch, sh, wh			___ /7
Frequently used Words Assessment	she's, who's, you're, unless, across, answer, its, answered, that'll, rather, again, shrieked, thought, through, demanded, although, enough, exactly, once, history, including, often, usually, within, examples, area, throughout, century, ideas, prove, included, order, otherwise, population, unable, colourful, least, million, similar, third, areas, feed, female, grows, stays, appears, proven, studying, survive, threat			___ /50
Comprehension Assessment	1. 2. 3. 4. 5. 6. 7. 8. 9.			✓/✗ ✓/✗ ✓/✗ ✓/✗ ✓/✗ ✓/✗ Valid/Invalid Valid/Invalid Valid/Invalid

Reading Record

The Contest Level 23 Silver

Name: _____ Date: _____ Age: _____

Text: ____The Contest____ Level: ____23____

R.W.: ____141____ Accuracy: _____ S.C. Rate: _____

Page			E	S.C.	Errors MSV	Self-corrections MSV
4	Arachne was a talented young spinner and weaver.	8				
	She had learned all she knew from her teacher	17				
	Athena, the Greek goddess of arts and crafts.	25				
	Arachne made the most wonderful fabrics and	32				
	tapestries that were not only beautiful, but were	40				
	used like paintings, to tell stories.	46				
	Unhappily for her, she was proud and stubborn, and	55				
	it was only a matter of time before she and the	66				
	powerful, and equally proud and stubborn, Athena,	73				
	clashed.	74				
6	That's lovely work, my dear.	79				
	Yes, I am pleased with it. I think it's the best thing	91				
	that's ever been done in this workshop.	98				
	What? Better than the goddess Athena's work?	105				
	Yes, look at this and tell me it's not better	115				
7	than Athena's work.	118				
	It's not a good idea to boast that you are better	129				
	than a goddess.	132				
	After all, she did teach you everything you know.	141				
Total:						

Reading Record Assessment

The Contest   Level 23 Silver

Name: _____

Reading level: _____

Accuracy level: _____ = 1: _____ = _____%

Self-correction rate: _____ = _____ = 1: _____   Easy/Instructional/Hard

Questions to Check for Understanding

Literal
1. Who taught Arachne everything she knows about spinning and weaving?   Yes/No
   (Athena)
2. Why is Athena angry at Arachne?   Yes/No
   (Athena is angry because Arachne thinks her work is better than Athena's.)

Inferential
1. What sort of powers does Athena have?   Yes/No
   (Athena can change the weather and can transform people into spiders.)
2. Why is it only a matter of time until Arachne and Athena clash?   Yes/No
   (It is only a matter of time until Arachne and Athena clash because Arachne thinks her work is better than the goddess's.)

Response
1. Do you think Arachne would win a contest against Athena? Why or why not?   Valid/Invalid

Analysis of reading behaviours (meaning, structural and visual information, self-monitoring, self-correcting, fluency)

_____

_____

_____

_____

_____

_____

_____

Phonics Assessment
Level 23 Silver

Name: _____

Age: _____ Date: _____

tea	skis	these
owned	float	though
world	twirl	whirl
awesome	draw	thought
daily	stay	they
you	truth	who
short	ensure	
large		
pair	flair	chair
here	clear	shear

Frequently Used Words Assessment

Level 23 Silver

Name: _____

Age: _____   Date: _____

although	enough	countries	keeps
around	thought	democracy	objects
brought	better	people	money
each	think	alike	already
knew	teach	government	lovely
before	month	different	beautiful
every	cheque	mothers	person
suddenly	using	later	account
walk	areas	together	cities
world	easier	two	coins
nights	discovered	against	public
slave	weapons	change	
because	history	reduce	

Comprehension Assessment
Fiction

Level 23 Silver

Name: _____ Age: _____ Date: _____

The Contest ✓ or ✗

1. What is the theme of Athena's tapestry? (literal)

2. What does Athena do to Arachne's tapestry? (literal)

3. What does Athena do to Arachne to punish her? (literal)

4. On page 9, what has happened to the old woman? (inferential)

5. Why does Athena say that Arachne has insulted the gods with her work? (inferential)

6. How does Athena show her anger when Arachne boasts that her work is the best (pages 7–9)? (inferential)

7. Do you think Arachne is sensible to challenge Athena to a contest? Why or why not? (response)

    Valid/Invalid

8. Do you think Arachne deserves to be turned into a spider? Why or why not? (response)

    Valid/Invalid

9. Do you agree with Arachne when she says that the gods are terrible? Why or why not? (response)

    Valid/Invalid

Silver Band Placement Sheet

Level 23 Silver

Name: _____ Age: _____ Date: _____

Fluency and Accuracy		Correct words per minute	Accuracy Rate	Self-correction Rate
	Text 1		%	1:
	Text 2		%	1:
Comments on the information systems	Meaning Structure Visual			
Reading Record Comprehension	Literal 1. 2.			Yes/No Yes/No
	Inferential 1. 2.			Yes/No Yes/No
	Response 1.			Valid/Invalid
Phonics Assessment	Phonic combinations to be learned long *e*, long *o*, /er/, /or/, long *a*, long *oo* sound, /sh/, /j/ = soft *g*, /air/, /ear/			___ /10
	Blends to be learned sk, fl, tw, dr, st, tr, en, fl, cl			___ /9
	Digraphs to be learned ch, sh, th, wh			___ /8
Frequently Used Words Assessment	Although, around, brought, each, knew, before, every, suddenly, walk, world, nights, slave, because, enough, thought, better, think, teach, month, cheque, using, areas, easier, discovered, weapons, history, countries, democracy, people, alike, government, different, mothers, later, together, two, against, change, reduce, keeps, objects, money, already, lovely, beautiful, person, account, cities, coins, public			___ /50
Comprehension Assessment	1. 2. 3. 4. 5. 6. 7. 8. 9.			✓/✗ ✓/✗ ✓/✗ ✓/✗ ✓/✗ ✓/✗ Valid/Invalid Valid/Invalid Valid/Invalid

Reading Record

More Like Home   Level 25 Emerald

Name: _____   Date: _____   Age: _____

Text: _____*More Like Home*_____   Level: __*25*__

R.W.: _____*148*_____   Accuracy: _____   S.C. Rate: _____

Page			E	S.C.	Errors MSV	Self-corrections MSV
10	I had felt fear before. Fear had been a part of my	12				
	life ever since the soldiers started coming to the	21				
	village. But, now, I felt something worse – a deep	30				
	feeling of sadness and loss to be leaving my	39				
	homeland.	40				
	I'm tired.	42				
	Let's rest here for a while then.	49				
11	We woke at sunrise to the sound of a truck pulling	60				
	up nearby.	62				
	Quick! Soldiers!	64				
	My heart beat like a drum.	70				
	Shh.	71				
	We sat still, hardly breathing.	76				
12	Do you think they were looking for us?	84				
	I don't know, but they'd take us anyway.	92				
	Let's go! Quickly!	95				
	The soldiers often kidnapped children for the army.	103				
	I can't see anything, or anyone.	109				
13	We just have to keep going.	115				
	Then, just as I'd almost given up hope …	123				
	We're looking for the border.	128				
	You've crossed the border. You can keep walking	136				
	with us to the camp. We're all going to the	146				
	same place.	148				
Total:						

Reading Record Assessment

More Like Home   Level 25 Emerald

Name: _____

Reading level: _____

Accuracy level: _____ = 1: _____ = _____%

Self-correction rate: _____ = _____ = 1: _____

Easy/Instructional/Hard

Questions to Check for Understanding

Literal
1. Why does Grace's heart beat like a drum?   Yes/No
   (She and Moses see soldiers arriving.)
2. How does Grace know she has found people from the same area as her?   Yes/No
   (The people speak the same language as Grace.)

Inferential
1. Why is Grace desperate to find a face she knows?   Yes/No
   (She hopes to hear news from home.)
2. Why does Grace feel numb as she walks to the border?   Yes/No
   (She has just heard that her village was burnt to the ground, and that it is possible that no one survived.)

Response
1. How do you think Grace and Moses would have felt when they found people they knew?   Valid/Invalid

Analysis of reading behaviours (meaning, structural and visual information, self-monitoring, self-correcting, fluency)

_____
_____
_____
_____
_____
_____
_____
_____

Phonics Assessment
Level 25 Emerald

Name: _____

Age: _____   Date: _____

nest	crest	chest
bad	traditional	
imperial	impressive	
bun		shun
important		porch
environment	spent	when
experiment		
individuals		inch
retina		
part		parch

Frequently Used Words Assessment

Level 25 Emerald

Name: _____

Age: _____ Date: _____

allowed	farther	attack	touching
months	desperately	attachment	measured
aunt	laughed	suit	allow
quickly	middle	switching	eleven
language	strengthen	popular	greatness
afterwards	slow	bright	older
strangely	perfect	colour	systems
necessary	alternatives	excellent	lose
hour	current	perceive	bought
half	course	receive	own
touched	describing	caught	fewer
exactly	opinion	easier	
further	colour	loosens	

Comprehension Assessment
Fiction

Level 25 Emerald

Name: _____ Age: _____ Date: _____

More Like Home ✓ or ✗

1. What did Moses's mother tell them to do if it wasn't safe to go back to the village? (literal)
   _____ ☐

2. Describe the conditions in the refugee camp. (literal)
   _____ ☐

3. How does Grace react when she is told that they're going to Australia? (literal)
   _____ ☐

4. What happens to Grace's mum and her baby? (inferential)
   _____ ☐

5. On page 6, why is Grace not sure that she believes her own words? (inferential)
   _____ ☐

6. Why does Grace fall asleep in minutes once she's set up camp? (inferential)
   _____ ☐

7. Why do you think soldiers kidnapped children for the army? (response)
   _____ Valid/Invalid

8. How would you feel if you were forced to leave your home and go to another country? (response)
   _____ Valid/Invalid

9. Why might it be hard for Grace to go on a plane? (response)
   _____ Valid/Invalid

Emerald Band Placement Sheet

Level 25 Emerald

Name: _____ Age: _____ Date: _____

Fluency and Accuracy		Correct words per minute	Accuracy Rate	Self-correction Rate
	Text 1		%	1:
	Text 2		%	1:
Comments on the information systems	Meaning Structure Visual			
Reading Record Comprehension	Literal 1. 2.			Yes/No Yes/No
	Inferential 1. 2.			Yes/No Yes/No
	Response 1.			Valid/Invalid
Phonics Assessment	Phonic combinations to be learned est, ad, im, un, por, en, ex, in, re, par			___/10
	Blends to be learned cr, tr, pr, sp			___/4
	Digraphs to be learned ch, sh, wh			___/6
Frequently Used Words Assessment	allowed, months, aunt, quickly, language, afterwards, strangely, necessary, hour, half, touched, exactly, further, farther, desperately, laughed, middle, strengthen, slow, perfect, alternatives, current, course, describing, opinion, colour, attack, attachment, suit, switching, popular, bright, colour, excellent, perceive, receive, caught, easier, loosens, touching, measured, allow, eleven, greatness, older, systems, lose, bought, own, fewer			___/50
Comprehension Assessment	1. 2. 3. 4. 5. 6. 7. 8. 9.			✓/✗ ✓/✗ ✓/✗ ✓/✗ ✓/✗ ✓/✗ Valid/Invalid Valid/Invalid Valid/Invalid

Pro forma
Reading Record

Name: _____ Date: _____ Age: _____

Text: _____ Level: _____

R.W.: _____ Accuracy: _____ S.C. Rate: _____

Page		E	S.C.	Errors MSV	Self-corrections MSV
Total:					

Pro forma Reading Graph

Reading Graph

Name: _____   Age: _____   Starting Level: _____

	Activity
Level 25	P C V W
Level 24	P C V W
Level 23	P C V W
Level 22	P C V W
Level 21	P C V W
Level 20	P C V W
Level 19	P C V W
Level 18	P C V W
Level 17	P C V W
Level 16	P C V W
Level 15	P C V W
Level 14	P C V W
Level 13	P C V W
Level 12	P C V W
Level 11	P C V W
Level 10	P C V W
Level 9	P C V W
Level 8	P C V W
Level 7	P C V W
Level 6	P C V W

Date

KEY
P Phonics
C Comprehension
V Vocabulary
W Writing

Pro forma
Weekly Individual Literacy Plan

Weekly Individual Literacy Plan

Name: _____ Age: _____ Reading Level: _____

Term: _____ Week: _____ Date: _____

Text	Area of Need	Strategies	Monitoring/Assessment	Comments

Making the most of Phonic Opportunities

All *Fast Lane* readers will test a pupil's phonic knowledge and skills. The following is a list of ideas for short, practical activities that will draw on and reinforce a pupil's phonic skills. They could be done after reading in a session with *Fast Lane*. Levels have been suggested, although many activities can be adapted to suit texts at any level.

Level	Type of Activity	Activity
6	Swap the consonant	Ask the pupils to use letter tiles to make a word in the pattern, e.g. 'hat'. Then give them another consonant (e.g. 'm') and ask them to take away the 'h' and put in the 'm' to make a new word. Repeat.
7	What word am I?	Play What Word Am I? Choose a word from the phonic opportunities list and give the pupils clues so that they can guess what it is. For example: "I rhyme with pink. I am used to wash the dishes. What word am I?"
8	Listen and clap	Write one of the words from the phonic opportunities list on the board, e.g. 'shop'. Ask the pupils to clap when they hear a word that rhymes with 'shop'. Say a list of rhyming and non-rhyming words, such as 'hop', 'ship', 'stop', 'shop'. Repeat the activity with other words.
9	Rhyming concentration	Ask the pupils to play Rhyming Concentration, in pairs. Make two sets of word cards, using rhyming pairs from the phonic opportunities list and the frequently used words list. Ask the pupils to lay out both sets of cards, face down. Each pupil turns over two cards per turn. If the cards rhyme, they keep them and have another turn. If not, they turn the cards face down again and the next player has a turn. When all the pairs are found, the player with more pairs wins.
10	Make rhymes	Help the pupils to compose short, two-line rhymes, using the words from the phonic opportunities list. For example: After school I caught the train, and soon I was at home again.
11	I went shopping	Say each group of words from the phonic opportunities list and the frequently used word list. Ask them to identify which part of the words sound the same. Play 'I went shopping' to further develop their understanding. Use items with the same phoneme for the shopping list, e.g. hand cream, peaches, beach towel, cleaning products.
12	Missing consonant	Write an alphabet strip of the consonants on the board. Write words from the phonics opportunities list which have one consonant missing, e.g. scree-, dow-. The pupils select one consonant from the list to fill the gaps to complete each word, i.e. 'n'. Repeat with other words from the text that have the same missing consonant.
13	Syllables	Make sure the pupils are able to break words into syllables and identify the number of syllables in words, e.g. pain: 1 syllable; medicine: med / i / cine: 3 syllables; company: com / pan / y: 3 syllables. Say the word 'company'. Ask the pupils to say the word, breaking it into syllables and clapping the syllables as they hear them. Give the pupils practice in breaking key words from the text into syllables as a listening and oral activity only. Break medicine into syllables. Clap each syllable i.e.: med / i / cine. Pupils repeat the word. Say and clap the word, omitting a syllable. The pupils must guess what syllable was left out, e.g. : medicine: med/i/_ _ _ _ . Pupils reply 'cine'; powder: _ _ _ /der. Pupils reply 'pow'

Level	Type of Activity	Activity
14	Syllable clues	Give pupils clues to a word in the text based on its meaning and the number of syllables, e.g. a 2- syllable word that means a runner who races over a short distance. (sprinter) Pupils say the word and clap the syllables. Give the pupils the opportunity to make up clues for their partner.
15	Prefix or suffix?	Write a root word on the board and ask the pupils build a word family by adding suffixes or prefixes. Responses can be oral or written.
16	Syllable groups	Write a list of technical and frequently used words on cards. Ask the pupils to read the words and sort them into groups according to the number of syllables.
17	Which word looks correct?	Choose a word from the text and write it several times – once with correct spelling , the others with alternative spelling patterns. (e.g. traffick, traffic, trafic) Ask, "Which word looks correct?" Ask the pupils to identify the word with the correct spelling.
18	Missing letters	Write words on the board with the last three letters missing. Ask the pupils to supply the missing letters.
19	Syllable mix	Write frequently used and phonic opportunity words on cards. Group the words according to the number of syllables. Ask the pupils to read the words, clap the syllables, then cut the words into syllables (i.e. fam /il /ies). Mix up the syllables and ask the pupils to remake the words. Can you make other new words using the syllables?
20	Syllable box	Draw a box on the board. Divide the box into two sections. Pupils locate a 2- syllable word in the phonic opportunities list and write it in the box, writing one syllable in each section. What other words could have fitted into this syllable box? Repeat with 3-and 4- syllable words from the word lists.
21	Homophones	Write, 'two, too, to; their, there, they're' on the board. Identify these groups as homophones. What letters represent the same sound in each word (what graphemes represent the same phoneme)? How do you work out which word you need to use in a sentence if they sound the same? Dictate simple sentences containing these words for the pupils to write.
22	Silent letters	Compile lists of words containing a specific silent letter: castle, listen, whistle, often; answer, write, wrong, wriggle; calm, folk, talk, walk.
23	Speed word	Set a time limit and select a letter/grapheme combination. Ask the pupils to write as many words as possible within the timeframe that contain that grapheme combination.
24	True or false?	Make a statement about syllables. Pupils decide if the statement is true or false, giving examples to justify their answers. For example, syllables usually have a vowel or a 'y' in them (true); some words have zero syllables (false); nt, nd, st are all syllables (false).
25	Common syllables	Break frequently used and phonic opportunity words into syllables. List words that contain common syllables (e.g. –sure: treasure, pleasure, measure; -tion: imagination, education, investigation; -ture: adventure, capture, picture, furniture).

Making the most of frequently used words

The following practical activities will ensure pupils recognise and secure frequently used words for future reading. The levels at which they may be appropriate are suggested, but these are only a guide. The most appropriate time for playing these games would be as part of the *After Reading* session; they could also be used as a stand-alone activity, if there is an available adult. To support preparation of these activities, lists of the frequently used words are provided on pages 34–51. The number of pupils working with an adult could range from 1-6, depending on the nature of the activity. To keep the pupils' interest, each activity should be well-paced and last for no longer than five minutes.

Level	Type of Activity	Activity
6-10	Pairs	Make two sets of cards with one frequently used or other known word on each card. Layout one set of cards, face up. Ask the pupils to select one card from the second set, say the word and find the matching card.
6-10	Fish	Play Fish in pairs. Use the two sets of cards described in 'Pairs' above. Deal five cards to each player. Put the remaining cards face down in a stack. The aim is to make pairs. The players take turns to ask, "Do you have the word (have)?" If the answer is yes, they collect the matching card. If the answer is no, they take the top card from the stack. The player with the most pairs wins.
6-10	Missing word memory game	Select four or more word cards and lay them out on the table. Ask the pupils to read the words and then close their eyes whilst you remove one card. Ask the pupils to identify the missing card. Repeat with other sets of words.
6-10	Random words	Make a set of cards with one word from the frequently used word list on each card. Use other known words as well. Say four of the words in a random order. Ask the pupils to take those cards and arrange them in the order in which they were spoken, then read the words in order. Repeat the activity with different words, gradually increasing the number of words to five and six. Then ask the pupils to select and read the words to be put in order.
6-10	Mind reader	Lay out one set of the cards of words from the frequently used word list face up. Provide clues about one word, for example: The word I am thinking of has six letters. It contains the word 'all'. Tell the pupils to 'read your mind' and write the word you are thinking of (called). Swap roles, asking the pupils to give clues to the words of their choice.
6-10	Word jumble	Jumble the letters of a frequently used word and write it on the board. Ask the pupils to say and write the correct word.
6-10	Which is correct?	Write a frequently used word twice on the board- once with correct spelling and once with incorrect spelling. Ask the pupils to identify the correct spelling and copy it for practice.
10-25	Guess in 10	Use known and new frequently used words. Select a word. Write spaces for each letter in the word on the board. Ask the children to guess the letters in fewer than 10 guesses to win the game. Record the number of guesses and letters used. Alter the number of guesses depending on the length of the word and the pupils' ability.
10-25	Strategies for memorising words	Discuss strategies for memorising words (i.e. reciting the letters, breaking the words into syllables, looking for smaller words, visual letter patterns). Write a frequently used word on the board. Ask the pupils to use letter tiles to make the word and then memorise it. Erase the word. The pupils then jumble their letters and remake the word. What strategies were most effective for memorising the word? Did the same strategy work best for everybody?

Level	Type of Activity	Activity
10-25	Spin the Pen	Using new and known frequently used words from previous reading sessions, write 20 words on cards. Place in a circle. Pupils take it in turns to spin the pen and say the word to which the pen points.
10-25	Sentences	Write three frequently used words from the text that can be used to make a sentence, e.g. teacher, laughed, school. Pupils read the words then use them in a sentence, e.g. The teacher laughed outside the school.
15-25	Missing vowels	Write a frequently used word on the board, omitting all the vowels. Ask the pupils to complete the word by filling in the missing letters.
15-25	Suffix sums	Write the root word of each word in the list. Make suffix sums, e.g. chop + s = chops; chop + ed = chopped. How does the root word change when suffixes are added?
15-25	Random Order	Write the frequently used words on cards. Say four of the words in random order. Ask the pupils to select and place the cards in the same order. Repeat with different words, gradually increasing the number of words. Swap roles.
15-25	What's the group?	Write each word on a card. Ask the pupils to divide the words into groups and justify those groupings. Collect the cards and make your own groups with the cards. Ask the pupils to decide how you have chosen to group the words (e.g. number of syllables; words with suffixes; root words; silent letter). Ask each pupil to select a word from the list and say something about it. (e.g. 'knew' has a silent 'k'; 'would' rhymes with 'could'.
15-25	Missing consonants	Write some frequently used words on the board with all the consonants missing. Ask the pupils to complete the words.
15-25	Riddles	Give riddle clues for frequently used words. For example, buy: my first is in 'bad' but not in 'sad', my second is the vowel in 'bus', my third is the letter between 'x' and 'z', my whole is something you do in a shop.
15-25	Finish the word	Make cards using these and other known frequently used words. Cut each card into two pieces. Place cards face down on a table and take turns to turn one card over. If the player can orally make a proper word by adding an appropriate beginning or ending to the card, the card is kept and the player has another turn. If not, the card is placed face down again. The player with the most cards when all are turned over is the winner.
15-25	Sentence challenge	Write words on cards. Show the pupils a word card and ask them to use the word in a sentence. Challenge the pupils by showing them two or more words to read and combine into a sentence.
15-25	Word search	Show the pupils a frequently used word. Pupils scan the text to locate the word as quickly as they can. First to locate the word wins a point.